# *Verda*

## *A Novel*

*Dianne Zimmermann*

Published 2023.



Printed in the United States of America.

Cover art by the author.
Cover background credit © Can Stock Photo/
©Sunnyshine and ©yilmazsavaskandag

ISBN 979-8-218136-92-5

Publishing Assistance
BookCrafters, Parker, Colorado.
www.BookCrafters.net

*I dedicate this book to my friends*
*whose never-ending encouragement*
*drove me on when the going got tough.*

# *Acknowledgments*

I wish to thank my earthly family of friends for all of their interest and encouragement in all of my writing endeavors. Verda, is a work of fiction and my eighth book. And I would be remiss if I did not express my gratitude for my magical spiritual guides and my Pleiadian star family guides from Alcyone, Pleiades.

# *Chapter One*

"WISDOM, I NEED TO SEND YOU and your crew back to Verda," ordered Serena, Wisdom's Galactic Federation's commanding officer from the Pleiades brightest and central star, Alcyone.

"Do I really have to go to Verda?" Wisdom asked with a slight frown that narrowed her youthful forehead. Her sparkling blue eyes dimmed a bit hearing the order, moaned, "It's such a hell hole." She stood rigid in slight protest as she nervously ran her long slender fingers through her long blonde hair.

"Yes, I need you there." Serena, an ageless beauty, standing tall with long auburn hair and serious green eyes, displaying a no-nonsense attitude, as she replied with an urgency to her voice firmly standing her ground. She did enjoy all the members of her crew and Wisdom was one of her favorites, as she was one of her most intelligent and brightest investigators. The women were in the majority and ruled the population of the Pleiades seven sister star system from their headquarters on Taygeta. The Aquarian feminine ruling women of the

Pleiades were ageless. They choose their appearance, and the very old appeared very young and lived as long as they desired. Women made up seventy-five percent of the humans on the Pleiades. The few men there were domestics, as the women ruled, creating and maintaining a loving and peaceful existence throughout the seven sisters star system of the Pleiades. Pleiades was a peaceful loving place because the women ruled with a gentle hand, which was just enough to keep it loving and peaceful. As the women of the Pleiades had observed life on Verda, and learned from observing, that the underground evil reptilians had surfaced there and were living amongst the humans. They infiltrated the population by stealing DNA from the humans and thereby created evil reptilian humanoid hybrids. They were heartless and without conscious. They scratched and clawed their way to the top of the heap of society rule. They dominated the humans by creating misogynistic patriarchal rule over the humans on Verda. It all began thousands of years pass.

When the reptilian race was based on Lyra, the males had the females do all the governmental, commercial, and domestic work while the evil and conquering males went off to terrorized and conquer other star systems and planets. Over time, the males piled more responsibilities, work, and duties onto the females. And after a while, the females realized they were running everything; so, decided that they did not need the egotistical domineering males bossing them around any longer. So they became resentful and became rebellious.

The queen's team rebelled against the ruling males and chased the males out of Lyra. The males, having already blown up a few planets, had the Galactic Federation after them. So, when the women chased them away, they fled Lyra and went to planet Verda. There they hid underground, where they stayed and built cities and transit routes.

After the reptilian females cast out the males from Lyra, some females stayed on Lyra but many of the reptilian females ventured out and eventually migrated to the Seven Sister Stars system of the Pleiades and joined their fifth dimensional age of Aquarian feminine rule. They and many other women migrates from various star systems made up the female rule of the Pleiades. They were members of the Galactic Federation which consisted of about one-hundred fifty other star planets of the universe. Their goal was to stop the destructive forces of the evil, war mongering reptilian males, that were causing universal havoc and damage throughout the whole fifth dimension of the universe. The reptilian females of Lyra showed their strength and Galactic Federation worthiness when they took over the rule of Lyra and cast out the evil males.

The males then fled to human occupied planet Verda and went underground where they built cities and highways. But they swore in time to get even and retaliate the females for throwing them out of Lyra; since that time they hated all females and wanted to retaliate and one day create a patriarchal society on the surface of Verda. In order to do this in a clandestine fashion they needed to not appear reptilian. At the same time, the Galactic Federation wanted to rid the whole fifth dimensional universe of the evils of the reptilians, and wanted to contain them somewhere while they had the chance, so they quickly made plans to trap the evil reptilians on planet Verda.

In order to do that, the Galactic Federation quickly installed an artificial satellite moon over Verda to house a computer; and then installed a third dimensional producing computer on Verda's moon. The computer was programmed to create a third dimensional matrix bubble around planet Verda to entrap the evil reptilian males underground there.

So peace was once again restored throughout the universe. The plan was that the humans living on Verda's surface would not be harmed by descending the fifth dimension and experiencing the descending lower vibration of a third dimensional atmosphere on Verda. As the lower vibration of the third dimension was needed to entrap the evil reptilians there on Verda. The humans living on the surface had no idea that the reptilians were living underground; nor that they too were now trapped in a third dimensional matrix. The reptilians remained underground and built cities, and transit systems to connect them. But, then after a time they wanted to live on the surface, so the crafty underground reptilian males figured out a way to hack the moon's computer. Doing so they made life more rigid and toxic for the humans living on the surface of Verda, as the evil reptilians wanted to emerge from underground and live on the surface of Verda.

They hated and wanted to get rid of the humans living there, as the reptilians had claimed Verda as their own. The evil reptilians gained the knowledge from the computer which enabled them to learn how to steal human DNA from the humans on Verda, and so created reptilian humanoid hybrids that could easily shift change their appearance from reptilian to appear human. Then it was easy to infiltrate and mix and mingle amongst the human populations on Verda. The newly created reptilian humanoid hybrids had the ability to shift change and to appear human in order to rise up from the underground to the surface and appear human to blend in and mingle with the humans on planet Verda.

Although reptilian humanoid hybrids now had the ability to shift change and appear human, they had not gained the ability to acquire humans' emotions of empathy, love, kindness, decency and good well. They appeared human on the outside but inside they remained true ruthless and evil reptiles. They were evil psychopaths and sociopaths and scratched and clawed their way to the top of corporations and in positions of governments. They discovered they liked the taste of human flesh and formed secret societies to hold satanic rituals consisting of young, frightened flesh human sacrifices.

The reptilian humanoid hybrids lacking human emotions remained evil reptilian without conscious, heart or soul, performing evil and unconscionable torturous acts on humans. They hated all humans and set out to destroy them in clandestine and evil ways. They especially hated human females, since their own females had cast them out of Lyra. And in typical reptilian humanoid hybrid fashion they wanted revenge. In retaliation, they created a strict and rigid patriarchal society where all females on Verda would be considered enslaved second class citizens who would never ever gain fair and equal status to the males.

The reptiles were crafty and had taken the opportunity to hack the moon's computer when they discovered it was unguarded. The Galactic Federation had left the moon's computer unmanned when they quickly left the moon in their ships while it was still possible to leave to avoid mounting space debris. The evil reptilians had blown up planets leaving floating debris that was collecting and forming an asteroid belt around Verda. After the asteroid belt was formed, they could not send their spaceships back to maintain or guard the computer. So, Wisdom, a transforming human to spirit spy, had to be sent to Verda.

As members of the Galactic Federation, Serena, of the Pleiades, sent her best agent, Wisdom, to Verda to observe and report back. Wisdom could easily transform from human to spirit form and transport her spirit self to Verda in a nano-seconds. Upon arriving there, she could remain in transparent spirit form or appear in human form. She stayed in spirit form so she could easily travel about from nation to nation on

Verda, listening to leaders of nations' thoughts, and words and observing their actions.

It did not take her long to see the plans for global atrocities that the reptilian humanoid hybrids had to take place on Verda. They were already in progress and were being implemented in order to wipe out the human population on Verda. The invading reptiles had claimed the planet of Verda as their own and wanted to dispose of all the humans in ways that were not obvious as an all-out war would be. They preferred a more crafty, secretive, and clandestine mode of operation.

So the evil reptilian humanoid hybrids appearing as human, developed a fifth column plan, which was unsuspecting and appeared to the humans as beneficial and peaceful. The reptilian humanoid hybrids were psychopaths and sociopaths which appeared with a humanitarian facade to win over the humans. They hypnotized and brainwashed the humans to easily scratch and claw their way to the top of corporations and bought their way into governments.

To their disgust, they saw that the humans on Verda got along with each other, as they were kind, loving, healthy, youthful and lived long lives. This disturbed and angered the reptilian humanoid hybrids, as they wanted all humans on Verda to die and get off their planet. Verda was a pure and organic paradise and all the humans on planet Verda were in perfect health, and so the evil reptilian humanoid hybrids thought that they had to come up with a plan to make humans get sick and die. The evil reptilian humanoid hybrids proceeded with their viciousness and created havoc in many ways on planet Verda.

Their leading evil reptilian humanoid hybrid scientist team of Dewy, Cheatem, and Howd, developed toxic genetically modified organism seeds and had farmers plant them. Corporations sold the fake food products to all the food centers. The bad foods made the people sick. A wealthy oil man named Mockeferry, teamed up with scientists Dewy, Cheatem, and Howd, to create a medical system that served toxic drugs in the form of pills to be swallowed, and serums to be injected into humans with a hypodermic needle, all for their big profits.

Humans on Verda were not made up of chemicals; they were electrical beings matching the natural vibrations of natures. They were not by any means chemical. So when the food made them feel sick, the evil medical technicians were waiting with pills, ready to prescribe more toxins, not in the form of seeds but in the form of chemical based pills and injections. They were designed to make humans actually feel worse, because their immune systems could not tolerate toxic chemicals. Petroleum based polyethylene glycol, an antifreeze ingredient, mercury, aluminum, fluoride to name just a few chemicals used by the evil reptilian humanoid hybrids scientist team of Dewey, Cheatem, and Howd. Of course, Mockeferry had them add petroleum, so he could also reap the monetary benefits.

To promote their plan and make sure their plan was profitable, they bribed the media providers to promote the fake foods as being healthy foods. The evil reptilian humanoid hybrids created a toxic allopathic chemical medical system and waited for their food products to make the, once totally healthy, humans not feel well and to seek help. When the humans visited the newly created health clinics, the toxic pills and injections were pushed on to them. These toxic chemicals would be a sure way to a slow death when paired with the toxins the mad scientist had already sprayed in the air, water, and over the ever-growing fake food supplies. These toxic means were a way to weaken the human immune system further and make humans feel sick so they would go to the medical facilities to seek help; and there, being brainwashed and dumbed-down already by the toxic food pushing media, and not having any clue that they were being tricked, they willingly complied to getting pills and injections.

Their exterminating plans were going so well that the wretched reptilian humanoid hybrids in top positions of government, came up with even more vicious plans for the developing and marketing of fake foods. They developed agricultural agencies and created even more seeds that were genetically modified organisms that contained toxic chemicals made from petroleum. Planting these toxic seeds depleted the soil of nutrients and the runoff polluted the waterways. These toxic fake foods were not only sold in the nation of Malcatraz, where the idea originated, but sold in food centers all over the planet of Verda. Petroleum man, Mockeferry and his team of mad scientists, Dewy, Cheatem and

Howd, bought up the media air waves and pushed these products as they invoked methods to curtail and discouraged the sales of natural supplements and organic foods.

Slowly the humans were brainwashed and purchased more and more of the food products that had no nutritional values for the human body; on the contrary, they did damage. At the same time, the evil reptilian humanoid hybrids had created a fully for-profit petroleum chemical based allopathic health care system. The plan was very successful in making the reptilian humanoid hybrids very wealthy while wrecking the human immune system.

They pushed the sale of petroleum powered vehicles to cloud the air with toxic fumes. They dirtied the drinking water in all the cities with an aluminum manufacturing waste product called fluoride. And still more humans were being born rather than dying. The population of humans was growing not depleting. So the evil reptilian humanoid hybrids had to come up with another more vicious plan. They created wars, built hydrogen bombs, sprayed toxic aluminum chemical trails throughout the skies, and controlled the weather creating more frequent and intense weather patterns with storms that killed more humans. They concentrated more on their medical techniques making birth more unnatural and traumatizing to the human females, by using toxic pills and injections. And still the human population on Verda kept growing. They do not discourage the birth of babies, however, they found their way into the evil reptilian humanoid hybrids religious secret societies cults of human sacrifices of satanic rituals.

Then came the big plan.

# Chapter Two

USING FEAR MONGERING FALSE RHETORIC that a threat of a horrendous threatening disease was fast approaching, was just the added kicker to plant fear in humans. Worry and fear would quickly take down the human's already weakened immune systems. The evil ones triumphed in their success as they had established a successful for-profit medical system that falsely promised to return good health to humans.

Soon the people were coming into the medical facilities because they did not know what to do, as they were feeling bad. Being brainwashed, they could not put two and two together that their food and environment was making them sick, on purpose. All to happy and eager to come to their aid, the heads of the medical centers had their technicians ready and waiting for them with all sorts of toxic pills and injections. Injections were laced with toxic ingredients such as petroleum in the form of an antifreeze additive called polyethylene glycol. They also used mercury, aluminum and fluoride.

Fluoride was the waste byproduct of manufacturing

aluminum--what better way to dispose of waste, the evil ones decided. They even began upping the use of toxic fluoride, an aging, and bone marrow destroying agent, and adding it in the cities' drinking water supplies. The aluminum manufacturing waste byproduct of fluoride was increased everywhere in ever-expanding numbers. It was used in pills for mental health, dental practices swabbed it on teeth to "prevent cavities" which was a straight out lie. And of course, it was used in pills and injections in the for-profit medical system to further dull-down human brains on the way to their unknowing, and untimely demise. Fluoride was used in antidepressants to make humans more docile and compliant and easier to control during brainwashing programming.

The evil reptilian humanoid hybrid teams of Dewy, Cheatem, and Howd were becoming very rich, and the more money they made, the more they wanted to make, while on their way to ruling the planet of Verda and toward human depopulation. In the medical treatment clinics, the technicians falsely claimed that humans had very serious conditions that only their treatments of pills and injections could aid. They never mentioned the word cure, as there was no cure on their way to depopulating all of Verda. Rather, using toxic pills and injections claiming to help a human's depleting immune system; they further squeezed the life out of the humans in a slow deadly way that when they did die, their deaths would appear as death by natural causes, and be recorded as such.

To their evil pleasure, since they despised all women, they used the evil ways of their medical systems, when it came to having and delivering babies. Their hateful ways made it dangerous and unnatural for the mother and more convenient and profitable for the medical system. And so the reptilian humanoid hybrids' fifth column, clandestine, attack on the humans was appearing very successful toward ridding Verda of its nasty humans.

# *Chapter Three*

WISDOM COULD NOT BELIEVE what she witnessed on Verda, she was appalled at what she was seeing and hearing while observing the actions of the evil reptilian humanoid hybrids that had cheated, bribed, and connived their way into corporate boardrooms and to the top of government positions in all the nations on Verda. Seems the Galactic Federation made a huge mistake and underestimated the craftiness of the reptilian race when they installed the computer on Verda's moon and created the third dimension bubble that entrapped the evil reptilians, as they just merely turned around and made victims of the humans on planet Verda.

"Out of hatred for all humans, especially the females, Verda had become a strict patriarchal male orientated planet ruled by the males. They caused wars, and the once peaceful loving humans were hypnotized and brainwashed and turned their neighborly love into hatred for each other. The reptilian humanoid hybrids powers that be, were successful in destroying a once organic paradise, by poisoning the food, the air, the waterways, and they had succeeded in brainwashing the humans and made them obedient and compliant to their evil ways.

And now they had the humans believing that all of Verda was suddenly under attack and fighting a renegade highly contagious deadly disease. They claimed that in order to save lives and fight the horrendous disease that all must get injections, which was mandatory for their own good, so the media preached; and shamed the ones who would not go along with the mandates. And if shaming them did not work, they imprisoned them, tattooed them, and made a mockery of them. In the end holding them down and injecting them. Some were super sensitive to the toxins and dropped dead shortly after receiving the injections, but that fact was hidden from the public. Some had horrendous side effects of nervous disorders that caused constant shaking, and that was also ignored by the media and the medical facilities. Ignoring all that, they continued to order all humans to partake in the mandated injection program falsely promising to guard their health against the so-called deadly disease," Wisdom sadly reported to her commander, Serena. "Which in all actuality was not as dangerous to the humans as the toxic injections were. Truth be told, all evidence points to an all-out secret war on the humans of Verda," noted Wisdom as she updated Serena.

"I know, I received the earlier teleported updates that you sent," stated Serena matter of factly. "This is so appalling. The Galactic Federation has made a huge mistake by entrapping the humans along with the evil reptilians on planet Verda. I have also heard from Jules and Sally, our other secret agents on the ground who are working in a medical facility in the nation of Malcatraz, and they reported they are being threatened to get the mandated injections in order to keep their jobs, and to continue to perform their duties in the medical facilities there. But, their intuitions are warning them not to go along with it, and to quit their jobs instead, or lie. They could tell there was something very wrong about those injections; as they were seeing for themselves, that people were returning to the health care facilities sicker than ever before in their lives, after they received the injections," Serena continued.

"The injections were mandated and non-participants would be expelled from society and made to live in the trenches of concentration camps in eternal poverty. The injections the humans were mandated to receive were designed by men who appeared to be human; but we know better. We know that they are evil reptilian humanoid hybrids with conquering, hateful, and fear mongering dispositions. We know that they hate the humans, and we know that they have moved up from the underground to the surface of Verda and claimed Verda as theirs, and theirs alone. They want to get rid of most of humans on Verda, and save only a few to be used as slaves for breeding sacrificial babies for satanic rituals." Serena and Wisdom then waited in earnest to receive a report from agents Jules and Sally.

# *Chapter Four*

WORKING AS MEDICAL TECHNICIANS in the medical facilities, as Galactic Federation spies, Jules and her co-worker partner Sally's intuitions were correct. It was just as they suspected. It was not the supposedly contagious disease that was the real danger to the people of Malcatraz and all of Verda. Plainly, it was the toxic ingredients in the injections they have mandated all humans receive that was making humans sick and suffering horrendous side effects. It was plain to see that it was the evil reptilian humanoid hybrids' clandestine way to kill off the humans in a secret way that will appear be a natural looking death. But their head laboratory team of scientists, Dewy, Cheatem, and Howd, made the bioweapon, gain of function, spike protein injections too deadly, and the deaths came too soon after receiving them, so it did not appear to look like natural death--not to the global agents of the Galactic Federation members.

The injection recipients were dropping dead a few hours after getting the injections. Mortuaries reported a sudden forty percent increase in deaths. It was a vicious secret plan to depopulate the planet of Verda of humans, but it appeared as if the plan had gone awry and was too deadly; and so, they had to change the formula in the injection so the toxic gain of function spike protein worked at a slower rate. The humans had been brainwashed by the drug corporate-owned governments of Verda, which had bought up, bribed, and blackmailed the media to control what they reported and televised.

Jules and Sally discovered that not long after the first round of mandated injections, came a second threat, as the media bulletins interrupted regular broadcasting and told the people that there was another vicious variant of the same lethal disease rapidly spreading across the planet of Verda. They warned that everyone would get sick and die unless they got a booster injection, as that was their only defense against it and the only way to survive. The powers that be, discouraged the use of natural supplements and sunshine that would naturally build the people's immune systems. They prevented medical technicians from using alternative and natural treatments. Only their strictest guidelines were to be followe--those that were secretly toxic.

To make sure this was done, the health clinics were bribed and paid handsomely for following certain procedures, or be put out of business. But the Galactic Federation observed that even the bioweapon disease that they were spreading was less dangerous to humans; that is, if they had a healthy immune system, ate organic foods and took supplements. Of course, those things were suspiciously becoming scarce and ever harder to find. But the poisonous injections were readily available and were mandated, and the bought and bribed media pushed the injections and hid all immune building nutritional facts.

Wisdom and her team easily put two and two together and that was if the government was so concerned about humans' health, why had they been pushing toxic genetically modified organism foods to the people and continued to do so? Why did they not suggest the use of natural supplements to build up their immune systems, so they would not get the so-called dangerous disease that was so rapidly spreading? But as Wisdom and her team discovered, to prevent was not the case, but rather to sicken and destroy the humans was the obvious plan.

Sadly, the humans were already too brain fogged, hypnotized and brainwashed by the media to see what was truly going on. As it was, the toxic injections had horrible side effects that attacked the human immune system that ended up turning the immune system against its host. Many humans suffered serious side effects leaving them with horrible uncontrollable shakes; if they were not killed out-right after being injected. So many humans who were not out-right killed, were injured and permanently incapacitated, were unable to work, and forced to be on permanent disability.

Wisdom met with the Galactic Federation on Taygeta, of the Pleiades, and updated them, and requested that they intervene before it was too late. After all, they were the ones who had trapped the humans in the third dimension matrix along with the evil reptiles. The Galactic Federation was looking into slowing down Verda's moon computer. After the meeting special agent Wisdom, however reluctant, did teleport in spirit form from the Pleiades back to Verda, switching back to human form when she arrived. She continued her mission by investigating the operations of governments and of medical clinics and reported the information she discovered back to her chief commander officer, Serena.

"The people of Verda are being attacked by a threatening disease; but that's not the real threat. They are secretly being more dangerously threatened by the mandated lethal injections," reported Wisdom.

"Have you contacted the team of Jules and Sally?" asked Serena.

"Not yet, but I know at which medical facility they are working," answered Wisdom, "and I will infiltrate that facility now."

Wisdom would rather stayed working from home in her crystal lined spiral skyscraper apartment on Alcyone, the brightest star of the Pleiades, but she was proud to be a part of the Galactic Federation team and would happily carrying out Serena's wishes.

Wisdom was used to dealing with evil, as she had been busy chasing the evil destructive reptilians around the universe since they had been attacking and blowing up other planets. An opportunity had come up, when the reptilian females were left alone on Lyra while the males were off terrorizing planets. The females were left to manage the home base and take on all the responsibilities. After a while, the females got fed up with the war mongering males bossing them around, and they felt threatened--so locked out the males. Unable to return, the males fled to planet Verda where they went underground. The female reptiles remained on Lyra for a time, then migrated to the Pleiades, where they joined forces with the Pleiades women and the Galactic Federation.

The Galactic Federation, consisting of some one hundred and fifty star planets, learned that the reptilians were underground on Verda and wanted to trap them there on planet Verda, in order to halt their attacks on other planets. So they quickly installed a satellite moon on Verda, to house a third dimension generating matrix computer there. From the moon the computer broadcasted third dimensional frequencies surrounding the planet of Verda in a third dimensional bubble entrapping the reptiles on Verda.

The Galactic Federation left the computer unmanned as they were ordered to leave quickly. They had to leave in their ships right away, if they wanted to leave at all, because space debris was forming from blown-up planets the reptilians had destroyed. The debris was drifting their way and was quickly creating an asteroid belt around Verda. So Wisdom could only monitor the computer from afar. She discovered that since the computer on Verda's moon was unguarded, the crafty underground reptiles on Verda figured out how to hack it.

# *Chapter Five*

"It seems the evil reptilians that went underground on Verda have gone out of control and managed to hack the unmanned computer on Verda's moon. They created a way to shape shift themselves into reptilian humanoid hybrids by stealing DNA from Verda's human males, creating a special Y chromosome, so they can now appear as human men by shape shifting into reptilian humanoid hybrids and can infiltrate the humans on the surface of Verda.

So the reptiles now appearing as human have fully moved up to the surface of Verda. There, without human emotions, they are men who are narcissistic, egotistical and ruthless and have scratched and clawed their way into top corporate board rooms and government positions. They have managed to create a corporate owned fascist government. They have evil intentions to rid Verda of all humans so rules and policies were created to work against the humans. "These evil satanic reptilians had become even more aggressive and evil as they shape shifted into human looking reptilian humanoid hybrids," explained Wisdom to Serena. She added a bit of history as how it all came about when the reptiles were blocked from returning to Lyra by their females.

"When the reptiles first fled to Verda, humans were on the islands of Mu and Atlan and drove the warlike reptilians underground after they attacked their islands. Seems the reptilians were no match for Atlan's high-tech weaponry. The war mongering evil reptilians attacked Mu and wanted to retaliate and rid Verda of all human beings. Since the evil reptilians were no match for Verda's Atlan human technology, they came up with an idea. Crack the code to the computer on Verda's moon, that was placed there by the Galactic Federation in order to contain the evil reptilians on Verda, as the evil renegade reptilians were aiming to conquer the whole universe, and blow it up, one planet at a time. So the reptilians had to be contained somewhere. The Galactic Federation computer placed on the moon was programmed to hold Verda in a third-dimensional matrix indefinitely, which locked the evil reptilians there along with the humans. Blown up planet debris in the universe created an asteroid belt around planet Verda and made it impossible for the Galactic Federation to return to guard the computer on Verda's moon, once they had left.

Somehow, the reptilians figured out a way to hack the unmanned computer remotely. When they hacked it, they made life on Verda's third dimensional planet even more miserable for the humans. The reptilians figured out a way to steal DNA from the humans to create reptilian humanoid hybrids. They then had the capacity to shift change and appear human in order to infiltrate and mingle with the humans on Verda without them knowing they were truly reptiles. And of course, these evil ones ruthlessly scratched and clawed their way to the top ranks in corporations and governments positions around the whole planet of Verda." Wisdom extensively explained these facts from her research to Serena as best she could.

"Will the humans of planet Verda ever escape the imprisonment of the third dimensional matrix?" Serena wondered, "and will they ever be able to expand their consciousness and journey out into the universe back into the fifth dimension." She expressed to Wisdom her fear of what to her was an obvious no.

"Will the computer on Verda's moon programming Verda to hold it in the third dimensional matrix, ever break down, or will it hold them there for eternity?" Serena wondered aloud, but only time would tell.

# *Chapter Six*

"TIME WILL PASS. And the third dimensional computer on Verda's moon is wearing out and failing, so the third dimensional matrix will fade into non-existence. Only then will Verda be opened up and returned to the fifth dimension of the age of Aquarius Pleiadian feminine rule. The reptilian humanoid hybrids on Verda holding the humans in a prison-like state by manipulating and brainwashing them will eventually come to an end," Wisdom reassured Serena that the holding of humans mentally and emotionally captive in the third dimension would eventually end.

The computer on Verda's moon eventually will fail completely, and the evil reptilian humanoid hybrids will perish. Then the humans of Verda will be back in the fifth dimension with the rest of the universe. In the fifth dimension their bodies will become lighter and more crystal, the veil between spiritual and physical will be thinner connecting past loved ones spiritually with the physical humans. Love and kindness will prevail, and Verda's atmosphere will return to twenty percent nitrogen and eighty percent oxygen, back from the twenty percent oxygen and eighty percent nitrogen of the third dimension, which was harder on human bodies. Finally, humans will be free from the brainwashing of the third dimension and returned to the fifth dimension and join the rest of the universe.

"But it is not happening fast enough," complained Wisdom.

"I realize that, but it takes time," informed Serena. "The Galactic Federation is remotely slowly shutting down the Verda's moon computer."

"Can't they just turn it off," asked Wisdom, "and get it over with?"

"If they do that, the humans on Verda, will suffer mental problems, such as seeing scary ghost visions coming on too strongly," explained Serena. "This is why it is imperative that it shuts down slowly."

"I understand," answered Wisdom, "but the reptilian humanoid hybrids are becoming more angry and vicious in their efforts to rid the humans off Verda,"

"I know and that is why the Galactic Federation needs you there," explained Serena.

# *Chapter Seven*

"MUCH TO THE REPTILIAN HUMANOID hybrids disgust, the third dimensional veil was thinning, and the humans are becoming more spiritually enlightened and learning that their minds are all powerful, intuitive, and psychic. They are able to heal themselves and others via their loving vibrations for themselves and others. Many of the humans on Verda, who are suspicious of the powers that be, are taking it upon themselves to reject the evil reptilian humanoid hybrids power hold by forming resistance groups, led by many Pleiadians star seeds that have incarnated on Verda.

They are Pleiadian humans with star seeded souls incarnated there to fight against the Verda reptilian humanoid hybrid run medical industry that uses chemicals in the form of pills and injections to dumb down, manipulate and brainwash and eventually kill off the human population. But in spite of the reptilian humanoid hybrids efforts, the humans are continuing to be enlightened as the veil is thinning between Verda's third dimension and the fifth dimension of the universe.

Humans are learning that they can heal themselves and others with their loving thoughts and good intentions. They have meditated and learned to use their minds to rise above Verda's third dimensional veil to grow spiritually and expand into the spiritual freedoms of the fifth dimension," instructed Wisdom.

"I wish the Galactic Federation could just shut Verda's moon computer off now and end his madness," sympathized Serena. "End the third dimensional matrix, and Verda could return to its natural state that is in the fifth dimension." Serena was trying to find a way not to have to have Wisdom stay on Verda, as she knew she needed a break. She also knew that Wisdom was proud to be of service and would continue to spy on Verda and collect data, although she preferred working remotely from her home based job.

She monitored the energies of the universe from the comforts of her high rise spiral apartment on Alcyone, the brightest star planet of the Pleiades star system in the Taurus constellation. But she realized the reptilian humanoid hybrids on Verda needed to be contained as they were stepping up their plans to create more toxic havoc. They were brainwashing the humans with a threat of an unstoppable disease, so Wisdom would have to remain on Verda.

# *Chapter Eight*

THE REPTILIAN HUMANOID HYBRIDS in Verda's corporate owned government were warning that a vicious and contagious disease was rapidly spreading across the whole planet of Verda. So they announced to the humans not to worry that they had emergency injections ready, and all should get it immediately.

Only they did not tell the humans that the emergency injections were so rushed through and not properly tested. The reptilian humanoid hybrids ruled with fear and brainwashing. With genius trickery, nano microchip implantation was done by way of the injections; thus the fake threat of a contagious disease. The media did their part to brainwash the humans into thinking the injections were parliament in the prevention, or as a means to lessen the blow of the dangerous contagious disease spreading across Verda.

The vaccine was to protect against this disease that was determined to be of a dangerous nature; but turns out the real threat was the toxic injections that caused maiming and death, and yet humans were mandated to get them. So now the whole global population of Verda was in the midst of facing their possible demise. The public was lied to by the evil corporate backed fascist governments of most of the nations and zones of planet Verda. The highly lethal and clandestine project involved a threat of a dangerous contagious disease presented on the citizens of the countries around the planet of Verda, and the only way to survive it were the mandated injections.

Those who refused the mandated injections were tagged as treasonous and put into prison concentrations camps where they would remain until the evil reptilian humanoid hybrids, running the attack on the humans, decided to let them out. Or they were tattooed as traitors and then forced to get the mandated injections like everyone else. The injections consisted of a toxic concoction of polyethylene glycol, mercury, aluminum and the toxic derivative of manufacturing aluminum, fluoride.

The project was a global operation toward Verda's new world order agenda, consisting of a one leader program; the plan is in full force by the evil reptilian humanoid hybrids. All on planet Verda will lose their individual freedoms, be imprisoned as slaves and mandated to receive even more toxic injections. The insidious depopulation by toxicity scheme was solely created by three of the most evil shape shifting reptilian humanoid hybrids on Verda named Dewy, Cheatem, and Howd.

Their plan toward depopulation of the humans; is

to first, push bioengineering and create genetically modified organism toxic foods to weaken the human immune system. Then when they do not feel so well and go to a medical clinic they are met with a few questions, and merely handed a hand full of pills to take. And then, followed by a threat of a contagious disease, they are mandated to get a toxic injection for the final nail in the coffin, toward a guaranteed path to a slow unsuspecting death, that in the end, would be recorded as a death by the prolonged disease or by natural causes.

The media pushed the disease threat; so, everyone was in a panic and quickly lined up to be injected. A short time later, the plan continued to a second round, to introduce the threat an yet another variant of the out-of-control contagious disease, in order to mandate a booster injection. The populace was successfully brainwashed to expect more subsequent variants and more emergency fixes by more injections; which was expected to result in various life changing side effects, if not deaths, as the real threat continues to be in the toxic injections.

The third and final phase of the evil scheme was to turn what humans were remaining of the human population on Verda into docile compliant brainwashed slaves where mind altering brain control programs could be adjusted merely by sending various frequency signals to the nano microchips that were implanted in humans by means of the injections. This was the real reason humans were brainwashed and told that the mandated injections would ease the effects of the fast spreading contagious disease. The implanted nano microchips would turn all remaining humans into robotic slaves, as the humans were considered to be worthless, distasteful low-life creatures.

These ruling reptilian humanoid hybrids posed as benevolent humans. But in fact, these evil reptilian monsters saw young humans as tasty edibles, as they where evil, blood thirsty, flesh eating reptilian humanoid hybrids monsters in disguise. They especially preferred very young and tender flesh which was used in their satanic rituals.

Those who received the injections and had side effects were beginning to see the truth. Through the enlightenment teachings of the resistance groups, they learned to eat only organic foods, which supplements to take to build back their immune systems, and they meditated. They were slowly but surely catching on to the lethal scam of the reptilian humanoid hybrids. They realized the reptilians claimed they were first on planet Verda and that humans were unwanted intruders to be despised and disposed of. Also, through rules and the stripping of freedoms, it was becoming more obvious that the reptilians favored Aryan males and despised all minorities especially females.

# *Chapter Nine*

THE EVIL REPTILIANS DID NOT LIKE FEMALES because before they were cast out and landed on planet Verda, the reptilian race occupied the constellation of Lyra. There, they ordered their females to do all the work while the males were off terrorizing and blowing up neighboring planets. The males demanded more and more of their females until finally the females rose up and began retaliating. The disgruntled reptilian queen locked out the king and some other high positioned male reptilians. Out of anger, the evil male reptilians fled Lyra and ventured to conquer planet Verda.

Thereafter battling with the humans, they ended up sheltering underground, where they built underground bases and cities with high-speed transportation connecting them. The reptilians wanted to conquer the humans and take over Verda for themselves. So, the reptilians planned to gain rulership over the humans in a secretive clandestine way where the humans won't even know what is happening to them as the reptilians plan was to conquer and claim Verda as theirs alone.

In the beginning, the reptiles stayed underground, later on they decided they wanted to occupy the surface of Verda, and they wanted to rid Verda of the humans that were already there. To do this, they planned a way to infiltrate the human population in an unsuspecting way; in other words, to appear human and not look like the evil, and scary reptilians they were. So they stole some DNA from the humans and created shape shifting reptilian humanoid hybrids that looked like, and could easily pass for human males.

One thing though they could not inherit from the human DNA was a human sense of empathy, moral consciousness or benevolent emotions. In other words, the human heart, soul and consciousness did not carry over with the stolen DNA, so the reptilian humanoid hybrids were very evil, greedy, and ruthless, much more so than humans could ever be. So the reptilian humanoid hybrids were evil fear mongering monsters such as the pure blooded reptilians were. The reptilian humanoid hybrids hated all the human women especially, because of how their own females drove them off of Lyra, and they never forgive or forget.

The evil reptilian humanoid hybrids could easily shift change and appear human, except when they got very angry; then suddenly, uncontrollably their eyes would automatically shift change to golden vertical slits. The newly created reptilian humanoid hybrids, were just as the pure blooded reptilians were; aggressive, fear mongering, retaliating, and self-serving.

They were cruel and evil and swore to rid Verda of all

humans and to take over and make the planet of Verda theirs alone. After they began brainwashing through the bought-up media, the plan was first, to create toxic food and a toxic environment to weaken the immune system. Second, when the humans began to not feel well, and come to the medical clinics, give the sicken humans even more toxicity in the form of toxic chemical pills. Third, if they thought slow acting pills were taking too long, speed up the depopulation progress by presenting the threat of a fast spreading contagious disease, and then mandating toxic bioweapon gain of function injections forcefully and falsely stating to be the only option for survival of the dangerous disease. But just the opposite, the injections would lead humans toward an unsuspecting sickly, slow demise. They wanted human deaths to appear slow and spread out like deaths by natural causes so no one would suspect and catch on to their silent and deadly plans. It was natural for people do get sick and die.

Ironically, before the reptilians landed on Verda, the humans there were perfectly healthy. Part of the plan, was to brainwash the humans by buying up the media and spewing false propaganda. The evil reptilian humanoid hybrids smooth talked their way into corporate broad rooms and positions of government. Their media propaganda hypnotic and brainwashing techniques worked, and the humans believed whatever the drug corporate owned fascist government told them.

They became irate and were even willing to crucify

and ostracize the naysayers who separated and joined the resistance movement. Those who never, or had quit, taken in all the false rhetoric, along with easing off, then throwing out their prescribed and store bought toxic chemical pills, as they revolted and rejected the toxic chemical injections. They came to these conclusions and rebellious actions, after seeing how herbicide and insecticide laced genetically modified organisms were pushed on to the people as food when they are nothing but toxic empty calories made to attack and weaken human immune systems. Of course they were approved and pushed by the corporate owned government. The foods were full of chemicals without nutrition and so weakened humans' immune systems, setting them up for total health failure. The toxic injections only added more destructive measures to further take down the human body.

Very few people were catching on to the bad food scam. But those who were catching on and feeling as if they had been setup, thought that if you can't trust the food that was approved by the government; than how can you be expected to trust the medical systems' pills and injections? And if they really cared about the people; why did they not preach prevention such as eating organic and taking supplements to build up the body's immune system. They began doing more research and read where a guy, a reptilian humanoid hybrid, of course, wanted to depopulate toward a one world government.

Yes, that was the plan. The evil reptilian humanoid

hybrids wanted to depopulate the planet down to just a few million mind controlled and dumbed down slaves made so by toxic injections and fitted with an inserted programmable nano microchip. Another clue that some humans were catching on to the scam, was the ones who had managed to escape the evil propaganda and did not believe their bodies were made of chemicals. They believed humans are naturally made up of vitamins and minerals and are as organic as the soil, trees and all plant and animal life on Verda. So they rejected the false rhetoric, and therefore, maintained their excellent health, clear minds and perfect memory recall.

The reptilian humanoid hybrid elites on planet Verda were members of a secret ruling society, ruling from behind the scenes all the governments on the planet. They are referred to as the cabal, or the Illuminati, or the shining ones. These ruling reptilian humanoid hybrids could be easily programmed to honor, bow down, and serve the hierarchy of the elite cabal, the Illuminati. For centuries, secret societies have overseen the bloodlines and directed pre-planned and secretly controlled election outcomes. All was secretly manipulated from behind the scenes. The Galactic Federation had been observing and determined intervention was necessary.

The Galactic Federation high counsel commander, Serena, sent Wisdom to the prosperous nation of Verda, called Malcatraz, a nation claimed to be democratic republic nation of Verda. Wisdom dug deep into her research and learned that all the current and past leaders of Malcatraz, located in the Western Hemisphere of planet Verda, were related by an incestuous royal blue blood line stemming from an ancient dynasty of blue blood reptilian humanoid hybrid. A blue blood incestuous line that dated back centuries. These blue bloods were merely evil reptilian humanoid hybrids.

They sent their terrorist agents proclaiming to be explorers and claimed the land by fighting and conquering the native citizens of Malcatraz. When they were actually guilty of secretly murdering them by spreading disease among them to wipe them out, just as in more modern times. They did the same to the Malcatraz's small farmers by having them use toxic chemicals only to sicken them and wipe them out so big corporate could buy up all the farmland.

The clandestine fifth column secret attacks continued, and happening still, as the evil reptilian humanoid hybrids carry on their horrors to present times, clandestinely destroying human life through what they claim to be humanitarian acts but with a secret life destroying agenda. They operated their attacks by fooling and tricking an already brainwashed human population by circulating stories of a dangerous unstoppable disease and getting the injections would be the only way out of it.

Wisdom was not eager to face the obvious trauma on Verda. So she suggested Serena just have the Galactic Federation merely shut down the age old Verda moon computer, that projected a third dimensional atmosphere bubble around planet Verda to imprison the vicious reptilians there. Only problem though with a sudden moon computer shut down, is that it would increase human suffering--even more extensive since when the evil reptilians successfully hacked it.

The plan was to entrap and keep Verda in the third dimension, separate from the fifth dimension of the rest of the universe. And this was done from Verda's moon which was placed there to house the computer that projects the third dimension matrix bubble around Verda. If the computer was shut down, Verda's humans would no longer be in a third dimensional prison locked up with vicious evil reptilians, but back into the fifth dimension reset of the universe. The reptilians would be gone, as the reptilians cannot survive out of the third dimensional matrix.

Wisdom wanted the computer on the moon to be shut down to return Verda to the fifth dimension. But Serena reminded Wisdom that a sudden shut down of the computer, ending the third dimension, and putting Verda back to the fifth dimension suddenly, would be too much of a shock to the humans. They would begin to see ghosts and strange beings and past souls. Wisdom wondered how that could be any worse than being injected with toxic chemicals and having your life threatened, as they were experiencing now, and unknowingly being subjected to such tyranny.

Serena wanted to ease them out of the entrapment of the third dimension back into the fifth dimension, the dimension of peace, love and harmony. But Wisdom just wanted to pull the plug and get it over with. As she knew this tyranny was all a part of the reptilians' humanoid hybrids new world order's project to depopulate by the use of a secret invasion of disease onto the humans by their very own government. The current disease scam mandating lethal injections was killing people off at a fast pace, and Wisdom thought this needless maiming and killing needed to be stopped right away. She tried to persuade Serena to have the Galactic Federation shut down the computer.

"Serena, please order the Galactic Federation to shut down the computer on the moon now." Wisdom felt she was overstepping her rank speaking to her commanding officer in such a disrespectful tone, but lives were being lost needlessly.

"I have met with the federation, and the moon's computer is failing anyway and will soon die, but in the interim, we are decreasing its energy and shutting it down a little at a time," reported Serena.

Wisdom was only too happy to hear it. She only hoped it would not take too much longer as about a million humans across the planet of Verda have already died after they got the injections. Wisdom transported herself in spirit form throughout Verda, to pass through walls and ease drop on various government and business conversations. She overheard the head of a mortuary claim that deaths increased over more than twice as much compared to the normal rate of past years. And medical technicians were reporting when they performed autopsies, they were finding a strange long white rubbery substance that had formed in arteries and veins, alongside thick blood clots, too. And yes, medical records showed they had indeed received the injections. So there was something bad in the injections that was causing this strange phenomenon to occur. Medical technicians of course reported this to the government, but nothing was done to halt the mandatory injections. Wisdom reported her findings to Serena.

"If what you heard is true, and I believe it is," stated Serena with a clear sound of alarm in her voice, "this is an all-out war on the humans of Verda by their very own government. A silent war, which makes it even more criminal and horrendous."

"My fear is, Serena," said Wisdom, "that nothing will ever be done to stop them, as there is no longer any justice, or legal courts, left in all of Verda. The secret societies of the cabal and Illuminati made up of reptilian humanoid hybrids have successfully infiltrated every government in every nation of Verda, and they have been highjacked."

"This appears to clearly be an attempt of total human annihilation," Serena said in a strained voice.

"Please report my findings to the Galactic Federation," begged Wisdom.

"I surely will," affirmed Serena.

Wisdom than transformed from spirit form to human form to visit her fellow team member Jules, who had reported to Serena that she needed help as she was being threatened to get the injections at the medical facility where she worked.

# Chapter Ten

JULES, A MEDICAL WORKER, and just as Wisdom was, a human star seed from the Pleiades star system stationed on Verda to investigate suspected crimes occurring in government and in government run facilities. Just as Wisdom was doing, Jules was an undercover agent working for Serena and the Galactic Federation. Jules was appalled to discover the toxic procedures and injections that she was ordered to administer as she worked with the victims arriving at the facility with horrendous injection side effects, such as uncontrollable shaking and arteries and veins filled with strange blood clots that caused their bodies to shut down.

Jules' discoveries concurred with Wisdom's own observations. Jules told Wisdom that she was told to strictly adhere to certain treatment protocols and never to waver, or she would be expelled and blacklisted as an outcast never to work as a professional in the medical arena again. Jules had been mandated to comply to distributing the, dubious at best in regard to their safety, injections on all humans who were also mandated to receive them. She soon discovered that she was ordered not solely by the medical facility for which she worked, but the order came down from the toxic corporate backed, technocratic, fascist, government that consisted of non-human reptilian humanoid hybrids disguised as humans which were members of the cabal Illuminati. They controlled the whole secret depopulation agenda.

"These reptilian humanoid hybrid monsters have infiltrated and created corporate owned fascist governments and had blackmailed, brainwashed, bought up, and now controlled the health care system. They were calling the shots, no pun intended," Wisdom reported. "This is a deadly situation for all non-suspicions humans to be in. Most of them are already brainwashed by the derelict media corporations as they are all run by reptilian humanoid hybrids wanting to dispose of all humans in a way that makes it look like death by natural causes. Humans are brainwashed into believing that they all will get sick by a certain age and then die from illness as a natural cause of death."

"I figured as much," replied Jules. "I figured humans had been brainwashed, and lost their reasoning, as they seem to not be able to connect the dots, and put two and two together. They don't realize what is truly going on, and that they are under attack by their very own government. Anyone with a little common sense and in their right mind would see the lethal scam in all of this. Here's an example of what we hear in the medial clinics. A spouse may get the injection, and a few hours later drops dead of a heart attack on the kitchen floor, right in front of her, and their partner will never suspect the injection caused the death. I have seen and heard the same scenario repeated time and time again in the medical clinics."

"There must be nano particles and nano microchips in the injections," said Wisdom. "Get a vial of the injections serum, and I will have a member of the Pleiadian star seed team check it out in their lab."

"Will do," said Jules.

Jules and Wisdom shared the same fears that the plan was to implement total human mind control across Verda. They both witnessed zombie-like behavior of patients when they came into the clinics complaining about nervous shakes, foggy thinking. Jules and her partner and co-worker, Sally, were in horror at the eerie calm projected by the patients. It was as if they had come to accept their fate, and these patients had to be totally brainwashed and mind controlled."

"Yes, they are mind controlled by various media organizations that are owned and operated by the horrendous fascist government controlled by the reptilian humanoid hybrids who scratched and clawed their way to the top," Jules believed that wholeheartedly.

"Another thing, Jules," Wisdom whispered, "In spirit form I visited a mortuary and overheard medical workers saying that while performing autopsies they discovered tiny nano microchips that passed through the blood, pass the body brain barrier and were lodged in the brain of post injected human brains."

"So, I guess either the microchips controlled the

injected serums effects, or the installation is meant to control the human's thoughts. That is, if they should survive the brainwashing and toxic ingredients of the injections," stated Jules.

"Yes, and Jules, I overheard mortuaries chemist saying they found toxic chemicals in the blood from the injections. Toxic chemicals such as mercury, fluoride, aluminum, and polyethylene glycol, which is a petroleum product used in antifreeze. Oh yes!" Wisdom said suddenly becoming very alarmed and uneasy.

"This needs to stop, but how?" Jules stomach muscles tighten with fear for all the humans of Verda.

"What about you and the injections, are they still threatening you to get it, Jules?" asked Wisdom.

"No, because I and my partner Sally secretly falsified our records saying yes, we did indeed get the injections. We are sure many other medical workers here have done the same thing. Because how can we subject ourselves to the same torturous injuries we have witnessed coming in everyday to our facilities? We can plainly see the horrendous side effects, if not the sudden deaths, are plainly caused by the injections themselves."

*******

Serena expressed her gratitude as Wisdom shared with her the news that mind control was becoming more and more toxic to human health. All of them were being forced to be injected. She soon realized the real threat was not the proposed threat of the claimed wildly contagious disease, but rather it was becoming more apparent that injection injured patients were coming into the medical facilities within a few days or weeks after getting the injections. Somehow they never think it is the injections causing their problems.

Jules and Wisdom being on the front lines, reported to Serena, they discovered that the corporate scripted media broadcasting system was being used to mass hypnotize and brainwash the citizens. Not only the citizens in the nation of Malcatraz where her team was reporting from, but all over the planet of Verda. Serena was convinced it was a global conspiracy war on the humans, forced upon them. But why, they wondered?

Jules heard of AgendaX, a plan of a new world totalitarian rule that was in process, and it consisted of a depopulation plan. The depopulation plan was a conspiracy to create work outages, manufacturing material shortages, and food shortages, all on purpose so the evil fascist governments would take over, declaring martial law was necessary. They would go even further and confiscate everyone's life savings, their owned properties, move all the humans into cheaply built housing, and serve them Dewy, Cheatem and Howd's cricket and rodent protein for food.

Oh yes, besides forcing non-nutritional; poisonous genetically modified organisms, infused with toxic ingredients they want the humans all gathered into towering poorly constructed apartments in cities and fed crickets, roaches, and bugs for their so-called protein source. Of course, the creatures they were supposed to eat were probably killed by being fed or sprayed with poisons, which would according to plan also be poisonous to the humans who ate them. So it won't be long after that scenario begins to play out, that all humans will become extinct; just as the evil reptilian humanoid hybrids had planned it.

Suddenly, it all began to make sense to Serena; that, the real threat was not the disease itself. People could have healthy immune systems, by growing their own or by buying local organic foods, and not eating bad food or falling for the medical system's push on taking pills, which were just more of the same ingredients found in the injections. The real threat was not the disease but in the injections humans were being forced to get. And the injections worked fast; as the toxic serum bypassed the digestive system and was directly injected into the body. Faster yet, if they should hit a vein while injecting it, as then it spreads rapidly throughout the body and pass the brain barrier. The injections had toxic ingredients and many humans had strange and horrific reactions to those ingredients.

Jules saw many cases of constant uncontrollable nervous shaking of heads, bodies, and some with legs that shook so badly they were unable to stand, much less try to walk. Jules discovered much to her dismay, that the toxic injections were not meant to prevent illness, as claimed, but instead were meant to attack the immune system and turn the body's immune system against itself, which would eventually destroy it. This could easily be done because humans had already been set up, and their immune systems compromised and weakened by years of toxic genetically modified organism claimed as foods, that had no nutritional factors to them at all.

The people were tricked by mind control false advertising. And the bad food was everywhere and of course easily forced upon them because it was cheap and affordable to the people of Malcatraz. Greedy plans consisted of gathering all the money to the top upper echelon of the reptilian humanoid hybrid's secret societies. Jules felt that poverty was indeed planned for certain groups considered by the cabal Illuminati as undesirable humans. They were the ones to suffer most because the poor quality of foods had weakened their immune systems, making them more susceptible to negative reactions from the injections. Naturally, the sales of good healthy organic foods were in short supply or very expensive in most food centers, all by design of course.

Jules dug into the history of Malcatraz's health care systems and found that one particular foundation, the Mockeferry Foundation, was running and controlling the system to build up and channel funds to contribute to their organizations. The Mockeferry Foundation was into everything: medical, educational, banking and even the supply of petroleum energy for at least the last two hundred years in Malcatraz. The greed and desire for total control was holding back technical progress in Malcatraz because the elites were making huge profits and did not want to give up their profit building antiquated ways for the sake of humanities progress and growth. Verda was way behind the times of the rest of the universe, because of the selfish greed of the cabal of the Illuminati members such as the Mockeferry's and other narcissistic, greedy, and evil reptilian humanoid hybrids.

Through the years since the beginning of the last century, they had brainwashed and mind controlled medical personal, commanding them to push and force so called preventive pills and injections to the human population. Apparently planned as such, pills and injections were filled with toxic chemicals such as polyethylene glycol, an ingredient used in antifreeze. There was also toxic aluminum, mercury and fluoride in pills and in the injections. Why? Jules wondered. Years of toxic treatments were pushed by Malcatraz's corrupt government that ran the medical system, and were distributed all over the planet of Verda which had already weakened the population's immune systems. It was obvious to Jules that the humans of Malcatraz and the rest of the countries of Verda had been set up, by being served toxic genetically modified organisms in their food, and toxins in their pills and injections. All was a deliberate primer to get the population's immune systems in a weakened state and easily susceptible to further injury and death from even more toxins in the latest injections that were mandated by the corporate run governments.

That was the whole plan that was being successfully carried out and was now obvious to Serena's team on the ground in Malcatraz . It was a vicious tactic by the evil reptilian humanoid hybrids as a means to depopulate the planet by clandestine toxic medical methods. It was a blood clotting attack that would attack the human body over time and designed to look like a death from natural causes. However, autopsies revealed horrendous looking white clots found formed alongside thick long blood clots unlike any clots medical technicians had ever seen before.

So far it was being a successful tragedy that the fascist reptilian humanoid hybrid monsters had designed. It was an easy way to commit murder and kill off unsuspecting humans who could not even fathom their very own government's oversight agencies allowing this to happen. Per Wisdom, they were truly well aware but did nothing as the corporations owned the government's oversight committees. The medical and drug operations were run by the team Dewy, Cheatem and Howd, and they were in total control . It was part of the depopulation plan in preparation for, a reptilian humanoid hybrid's one leader, new world order, program on Verda.

It's to be a totalitarian regime run by a reptile king, in pure reptilian form, sitting on a throne, surrounded by human slaves, and ruling over all of the planet of Verda. The planet would be overrun and populated by giant lizard looking reptiles. But, in spite of all the secrecy, some humans were beginning to catch on and become suspicious.

So, the medical industry's talking heads kept

changing their claims from prevention, as it was becoming obvious that the mandated injections did not do that; so, they switched to a claim that the injections were making the illness less threatening. But medical practitioners like Jules saw that the spike protein in the injections seemed to be bringing on the disease and also stirring up other dormant diseases to flare up and attack an already failing immune system. And why not, as the toxic spike protein of the disease was found to be in the injections just as the evil reptilians humanoid hybrids had planned. The injections turned out to be more damaging than the actual disease itself which would have been easily warded off with a healthy immune system; that is, if the humans had healthy immune systems. But, with non-nutritional foods produced and forced onto them, their immune systems were sufficiently depleted to fall prey to the treasonous, attack by the governments on their very own citizens, just the ways of an evil reptilian humanoid hybrid government.

Non-nutritional foods, and the bone degrading aging factor of toxic fluoride was added to the water systems and required to be used in medical and dentistry use. The buildup of toxic pills and injections human bodies had received over time, had an accumulative negative effect, so had already taken its toll on their immune systems. It was a vicious and genius plan created by the evil reptilian humanoid hybrids who had scratched and clawed their way up into high corporate and government positions to set their plans into play.

The overseeing federal medical system had specific procedures and they demanded that all medical facilities personnel follow them, without exception, or be persecuted and possibly have their very lives threatened. Those medical personnel who struck out on their own and used nutritional type treatments that actually helped the patients, were expelled and cast out never to work in the medical field again. They were held down by government agents and forced to receive the very injections they were becoming more and more afraid of.

Jules tried to get out of getting the proposed series of injections by saying, she thought she was allergic to polyethylene glycol which is a toxic petroleum antifreeze and lubricant product that is used in pills and as a preservative in injections. Jules also was in the habit of reading all labels and discovered, to her dismay, that polyethylene glycol was even used in many foods products such as pastry items baked and sold in food centers. Jules thought she could lie too, why not, since she had been investigating and discovered corporations have been lying about authenticity and safety, and bribing government officials for years to get their toxic drugs approved. Through her endless secret research, she had discovered the types of contagious disease the governments were warning people about were diseases that were actually manmade and created in labs as bio-weapons, and had accidentally on purpose, escaped the lab, went airborne and spread amongst the people.

The injections were rushed and distributed and never

fully tested to know if they were safe enough to be used on humans. So neither the short term nor long term side effects if any were known. Soon, the effort went global, and all the humans of planet Verda were being mass mind controlled and manipulated to be in fear of a wildly contagious disease and told that only their injections could treat. Humans were being hypnotized and brainwashed through the corporate owned and bribed media, and therefore easily agreed to be injected with an newly developed, never used before, unknown new experimental, mRNA spike protein injection that altered a human body's DNA. At the very least, heart problems and side effects occurred in many of the those who received it.

"I have an update," declared Jules reporting to Wisdom. "I have discovered the injections are a gain of function bio-weapon, mRNA system newly created, poorly tested, and never before used on humans." Jules said that working in a medical facility, she had witnessed many patients suffering with awful side effects after receiving the injections. Some never had a chance to get to a medical facility as they died on their way home of a heart attack shortly after receiving the injection. A new term was created by medical technicians: "Vacaccidents," as more auto accidents were happening by injected individuals.

"This is appalling news," said Wisdom.

"It's like a war out there." Jules could no longer hold back her fear and anger at what appears as war on the people by their very own government.

"Don't you think that the Galactic Federation needs to hover their space crafts over the capitols of the countries of Verda, as a warning, to stop this vicious attack?" Jules ranted on, "The government should force a stop to the injections, but that is not happening." Jules was adamant in her belief that a warning by a show of alien space crafts hovering over the federal capitol buildings would be the best warning to put an end to this madness.

"Let me bring it up to Serena and the Galactic Federation council," suggested Wisdom.

After a while, Jules began to notice that the humans were beginning to catch on that they were mere tests subjects. Test subjects that were victims of the mad scientist of the globalist depopulation mindset that was apparently hell bent on depopulating planet Verda of most of its humans. The great reset plan had even been published so everyone could read about their agenda if they chose to. Jules read it and was appalled to learn that after depopulating most of the humans of Verda, the remainder of them would be nano microchipped and programmed as slaves to do the bidding of the evil reptilian humanoid hybrid elitist. Most medical personal were blackmailed to play along with the plans of the human destruction orders that were handed down from the very top echelon of the corporate owned government.

Galactic Federation inspector Jules was a dedicated and tireless medical worker gathering information while working secretly as a Galactic Federation spy.

Jules had reported early on to Wisdom, that she was in a precarious situation and would she come to help.

Poor Jules was being ordered to get injected repeatedly by her superiors at the medical center where she worked. Time after time, Jules tried to talk her way out of receiving the series of inoculations, she repeatedly swore that she was allergic to certain ingredients that went into the injections, such as polyethylene glycol, mercury, aluminum, and its manufacturing waste product, fluoride. Jules did the research and learned that polyethylene glycol was a toxic residue derived from petroleum. Jules saw how evil the greedy reptilian humanoid hybrid globalist cabal were, and guessed that the oil producers wanted to get their share of the profits too; therefore, polyethylene glycol was in the injections. Because the oil producers were so greedy, they also wanted to get their cut of the pill and injection action; so, they insisted that all pills and injections contained polyethylene glycol as a preservative and as a delivery system, along with the other ingredients of aluminum, fluoride, mercury and a programmed nano microchip.

The nano microchip was added in order to send certain frequency messages to the humans to make them docile and dull down their brain's activities. The reptilian humanoid hybrids working as general managers and controlling the corporate owned government wanted the populate sedated so as the humans would not become hostile and rise up and protest against the government. The plan was not to just dumb down only Malcatraz's population but reduce every countries' populations on planet Verda. Jules had discovered this and reported it to Wisdom.

Jules was appalled to think the very government was obviously in cahoots with and allowing big corporations to attack, maim and kill off the population. This was being done by the elite corporate heads and bankers who were members of the cabal of globalists who were gearing up towards their new world one dictatorship order agenda. The plan was that the planet's whole population would be dumbed down and brainwashed via their bought up and owned fake news media. The headlines were huge and frightening swearing that the populace was being alerted and warned that a dangerous disease was circulating around the planet of Verda and that only their injections would work against its spread. Jules discovered in a short period of time after the pandemic began, that the corporate own media was declaring that Malcatraz was especially hit hard by the fast spreading highly contagious disease. She suspected it was just more of the same widespread propaganda to get more humans in line for the injections and to lead the way for more strict government actions.

Warnings of such as these only gave rise to the dictator type demands of getting even more injections, living in isolation, experiencing loss of work, and the disabling of many public services. All group gatherings and small businesses were ordered to close down, and all court jury trials were cancelled, and citizens were stripped of a trial by their peers. Students were forced out of group gatherings and ordered to stay at home in isolation.

Jules had come to realize that she had been mistaken to think that the country of Malcatraz was still a free democracy. It was no longer free. She feared democracy would be lost forever. She was beginning to see the truth behind what was truly going on. Seems there was a newly placed evil agenda that was planned to not help citizens, but to contribute and speed up their demise. And all to be done to fulfill the cabal's goal of depopulating Malcatraz and the other countries of Verda from seven billion to one billion citizens on the whole planet of Verda. Those who survived, and were left behind alive, were to be turned into docile, dumbed down, programmed, slave experiments.

The head of the Verda world economic forum committee said those few million or billion humans left on planet Verda were to be programmed as slaves to serve Verda's high commander once the sole emperor was put in charge of Verda's new world order dictator rule. Evil lurked in the soulless, heartless, evil brains of a hand full of evil reptilian humanoid hybrids who managed to rise up to the surface from the depths beneath the crust of planet Verda and take over.

And it all began centuries past, that whenever the elite thought the population grew too large, they would not promote birth control methods but instead initiate a war or create a famine to depopulate the nasty humans as the reptilian humanoid hybrids royals ruling Verda saw humans to be lesser than deserving of life; they were a mere annoying nuisance. And now it was that time again, as the elite thought the population grew too large, and it was time to depopulate; this time on the largest scale agenda than ever before.

Wars that were used in the past to depopulate were too obvious and too expensive; the cabal realized that deceit and trickery was so much cheaper and mass mind control was now easier via modern day technology and the media. The cold heartless reptilian humanoid hybrids wished to erase most of humanity from the surface of Verda. Such was the goal, as the pure evil reptilians were self-proclaimed owners of planet Verda. And they wanted their planet, Verda, solely all to themselves.

Jules investigations revealed that the evil reptilian humanoid hybrids had infiltrated every corporate head position and had infiltrated every branch of the government of Malcatraz. They ran things for themselves from behind the scenes and saw that laws got passed favoring huge corporations. Even the oversight committees were bought, paid for, and brain washed to turn a blind eye to the toxic pills and injections that were being mandated onto its citizens, all in the name of making huge profits for themselves while depopulating the planet. Jules' mission was to pose as a health care technician at a medical facility, and now she has noticed something new that was occurring that she never had to endure before in her career.

"Wisdom, I need your help," pleaded Jules using mind to mind telepathy to communicate with Wisdom, "they are threatening to inject me with another newly developed experimental drug."

"I am on my way," answered Wisdom telepathically. Mind to mind is how the Pleiadians of the fifth dimension communicated, they could also teleport themselves in spirit form, so Wisdom using her mind, just thought about where she wanted to be, and then just showed up there, right by Jules' side, in seconds appearing in human form.

Never before in her medical career was Jules ever under such a threat. Now, she found herself threatened that if she did not comply to being injected, besides losing her job there at the medical clinic, she would also be black-balled from any other medical facilities within a hundred mile radius. But she feared for her life and thought she would be killed before she got a chance to warn the citizens of Verda and expose all the evil doings and trickery of the reptilian humanoid hybrids' regime that was in control. As a Pleiadian spy infiltrated into the medical system on Verda, she had to play along and follow all the necessary protocols in the medical system to not be suspected and expose her cover.

She had attended medical schools in Malcatraz so she along with the many other medical students felt the stress of being deeply entrapped by the weight of a huge education debt. The pressure of deep debt to enslave medical students was the whole point and goal of big drug companies and the associated funding facilities to rope them in, so they couldn't quit. Big drug companies set the agenda and running of programs of the medical teaching institutions in Malcatraz, which was overseen by the Mockeferry Foundation which ran the education programs.

The foundation also ruled the medical systems and financial institutions of Malcatraz, so it was truly a hidden technocratic dictatorship. The apparent goal was for students to be enslaved in debt for most of their adult lives. Stuck in deep debt was the plan to force medical workers into servitude positions, where they are so deep in debt they are forced to comply to evil and deadly tactics in order to keep their jobs so they could pay off their huge education loan debt.

Jules found that she had to continue working there even though she was fearful for her health messing with pharmaceutical chemicals on a daily basis. Toxic chemicals were found in everything surrounding her in the for-profit medical field. The medical industry in Malcatraz contributed largely to the prosperous capitalist economy of Malcatraz. With a population of about a five hundred million people, the economy was held up by their medical industry profits. Humans were mere disposable collateral damage towards their huge profits. Jules believed that the financial leaders running Malcatraz realized that since petroleum use was slowly going away and switching to total electrical power, which was cheaper and cleaner. Therefore, future big monetary gains would be forced to come from the health care industry. New power resources would have to be looked into--more natural, and nonpolluting to the atmosphere of Verda.

Perhaps the giant pyramids created by the extraterrestrials in ancient times and situated around Verda would be reignited to provide free electrical power for the whole planet of Verda as the aliens of old had intended them to be used. But greedy reptilian humanoid hybrids like Mockeferry shut them down and hid the technology, just so he alone could make huge profits and hold all of Verda in his grasp. But with their greedy minds set in stone, the reptilian humanoid hybrids petroleum agents, instead of switching their equipment to free pyramid power, solar and wind, were steadfast in their old oil antiquated ways, just for their own greedy profits alone. They stuck to the reptilian humanoid hybrid agenda tactic of, if you own the power and own the food, you own and control the humans.

So the Mockeferry Foundation was determined and willing to go to war and fight to keep oil as the priority vehicle for their monetary system, and its why they insisted polyethylene glycol, an oil product used in antifreeze, must be in used in every pill, injections, and even in commercially prepared baked goods. But that was for another time, right now, there was some sort of what they claimed to be, a contagious disease spreading at warp speed around the planet of Verda.

A deadly illness was created by the three mad scientist reptilian humanoid hybrids, Dewy, Cheatem and Howd. And these three self-proclaimed geniuses also created the toxic injections mandated on the populace by claim that it would halt the spread of the awful contagious disease. These three crooked, evil, tax evading, and very wealthy reptilian humanoid hybrid creatures owned the government that ruled the injections be distributed to the public in an emergency status. They owned the government via sacrificial satanic ritual blackmail and therefore protected by law to not be arrested for murder, sued, or made liable in any way for injuries or fatalities caused by the injections. It was truly a war on the people by the evil powers that be.

"It's brilliant on their part, isn't it," stated Wisdom after Jules reported her findings to her.

"Yes, it is," Jules had to admit, "first you create toxic pills, and toxic non-nutritional foods, that weaken and prime the human immune system. Then when the humans feel sick, they go to the medical facilities with health complaints and are prescribed toxic pills with more of the same toxic ingredients! Its genius, and something as evil as only psychopaths and sociopaths would execute. And to make sure the plan works, through religion, education, corporate owned media you brainwash and frighten people and tell them a vicious disease is rapidly spreading. The humans are already programmed to be fearful as fear and worry further wreck their immune systems. With the stage then all set, you go in for the kill, with the mandated toxic injections, oh yeah, it's genius alright!"

"Yes, I can plainly see we are dealing with crazy mad scientists," said Wisdom, "made up of non-human evil entities without souls or a moral consciousness."

"What about the law, the legal courts, will they go

after and prosecute the team of Dewy, Cheatem and Howd?" asked Wisdom, already knowing the real answer to that question would be a plain and simple, "no."

"The corporation heads have aligned the courts with their own evil bribed reptilian humanoid hybrids, so no, they will get away with this atrocity and even worse atrocities to come in the future, until all humans have perished off the face of planet Verda," sighed Jules. "What is most disturbing to me," added Jules, "is that they made all medical personal, accomplices to these obviously horrendous and murderous crimes. And they did so merely by blackmailing them as all medical personal were too deep in educational debt to just quit and walk away. But where is the consciousness and the hearts of these people? Have they been brainwashed while in medical training, or are all the male medical officials and attendees, reptilian humanoid hybrids?"

"Okay, let's break this evilness down," suggested Wisdom. "The reptiles hate females, so they were not used, so the male reptilians stole human male DNA from human bone marrow to produce the human male Y chromosome, and in a lab dish they probably added a few extra secret chemicals. Then the reptiles reproduced their male reptilians with some added human male Y chromosome and birthed reptilian humanoid hybrids in the lab. And these reptilian humanoid hybrids had the means to shift change their reptilian appearance to look totally human. And the only clue to these transformed monsters while they are appearing human is a possible uncontrollable twitch that leads to a switch from human looking eyes to a reptile's yellow vertical slit eyes."

"These three evil reptilian humanoid hybrids, Dewy, Cheatem, and Howd have brainwashed the humans through the media," explained Jules. "They brainwashed the humans to believe they are heroes when they suddenly came up with a miracle mRNA gain of function injection that they claimed would put a halt to the ravishing disease."

"Yeah, but which gain of function? The disease's function or gaining the function of the human immune system, so they can no longer fight off diseases as the immune system turns on itself, and ends up killing the human host," wondered Jules.

They both came to the conclusion that this clandestine attack on the humans had been in the planning for years, ever since they came up with turning organic crops toxic by genetically modifying organisms and by adding chemicals to the plant seeds, and then giving the plants a fresh dose of sprayed chemicals right before they are harvested. These mad scientists have developed toxic genetically modified organisms and passed it off as food in order to weaken the human defense immune system. Jules continued to explain.

"The idea was to have everyone get the injections," explained Jules. "So, they had the government mandate the injections in order for the citizens to be out in public and to keep their jobs. The truth being however, is the real danger is in the so called fix, the injection itself. So, if it was mandated, that made sure that a majority of the citizens were injected and would soon get sick and be drawn into the medical system. It was merely a way to drum up business for the medical system, before they possibly succumbed to the injection's lethal side effects."

"I think the scientists made some of the batches too toxic, as some humans were dropping dead hours after getting them," concluded Wisdom after hearing Jules' reports. "Apparently, they did not count on polyethylene glycol already being in so many prescribed drugs, over the counter pills, and foods; and that people already had an allergic build up to it. That is why, some injection recipients soon dropped dead of anaphylactic shock after getting the injections. Of course, the medical industry controlled media did not report that or warn the people about possible sudden death occurring after receiving the injections. After all the program is designed to depopulate. Right?"

"What can we do about this, Wisdom?" asked Jules. "This cannot continue."

"We need to call in the troops," answered Wisdom.

"There's more," Jules went on to further explain, "these three evil reptilian humanoid hybrids, Dewy, Cheatem and Howd, swore through the media that their injections were safe and the only way to be saved from this highly contagious fast spreading disease, was to get the injections. They swore their way was the only sure way to control the outbreak. And of course, to add huge profits to their portfolios. They made it so that every other natural or organic treatment was strongly discouraged by threats of fines, dismissal, and even threats on medical personnel's lives, if anyone should choose to practice outside the strict directive government posed guidelines established by the team of Dewy, Cheatem, and Howd. The plain and simple truth was that this is a clandestine war on the people of planet Verda.

The dangerous contagious disease propaganda was mostly just that, a scare tactic, so people would willingly stand in line to get the injections. The disease itself posed no real threat to a healthy immune system; one that was supported by lots of sunshine, rest, taking supplements, and eating only healthy organic foods.

Jules informed Wisdom that she had found that most citizens with a slightly less healthy immune system, meaning they already have ailments, got the disease for sure, after they had been injected with the spike protein. The spike protein continues to mutate in the body, spiking artery and veil walls, and causing blood clots. So the injections were planned for gain of function of the immune system; in other words, ruin it. Autopsy technicians found long strands of white rubbery substances, along with thick blood clots. The white stuff was a substance they had never seen before.

Between the horrendous deadly blood clots and the revved up immune system that never shuts off, until it finally attacks the human host and eventually destroys the human body, it's a perilous time. So, they were not surprised that humans were having stokes or dropping dead just hours or days after receiving the injections.

Seems that the injections kept the immune system revved up in high gear until it eventually turned on its own body. Those who had a healthy immune system and did not get the lethal injections fared much better when it came to fighting off the disease. Jules and Wisdom reported their findings to Serena.

"Only evil genius reptilian humanoid hybrids could come up with this secret bait and switch attack on the people," noted Serena when Jules and Wisdom reported the information to her.

"Evil and genius is correct," said Jules. "They have everyone propagandized into believing the government's constant messaging is in the human's best interest. People who doubt their motives and try to speak of their concerns about these matters are harassed by their brainwashed friends and families and further ridiculed socially as traitors, of all things. When it's clearly the corporate influenced fascist government that sold their citizens down the river of doom," she continued.

"Many humans caught on and realized the real threat, but it was much too late for most of them when they realized the health threat was the injection itself, and they had already been injected. It was why I did not say anything to any who had already gotten the injections--it cannot be ungotten, so why put negative thoughts in their minds that would only trigger negative thoughts and work against them. It was better to merely suggest rest, sunshine and supplements.

"The injection was quickly developed and rushed

out without thorough testing; and it was mandated to be injected into the arms of every unsuspecting human. The uninformed who were not suspicious by nature, had no idea that the injection delivered a dangerous spike protein that would mutate in the human body, and spike into interior veins and artery walls, causing blood flow blocking clots," Jules said.

"Well, I found out that most governments and medical facilitates began injection mandates as persuaded by the for-profit corporate controlled government." Wisdom then went on, "Three dangerous reptilian humanoid hybrid self-proclaimed top scientist named Dewy, Cheatem and Howd were determined to carry out the project at warp speed."

"And they are succeeding," remarked Serena. "Besides the bad foods, toxic injections and pills, as if that wasn't enough, for an added measure, Dewy, Cheatem, and Howd, fellow members of the cabal, thought for an added measure they would spray toxic chemical clouds through the skies with drones, all done in order to quicken the end of human life on Verda. The chemical trails were made up of aluminum and other toxic chemicals and sprayed in the sky all over the whole planet, in order to further weaken human immune systems to prep the citizens of Verda to be more easily receptive to the toxic injections side effects."

Every day Serena, Jules and Wisdom observed thick billowing white clouds forming in the skies above. Long lines of white fluffy thick clouds crisscrossed the once crystal blue skies of Verda. Even the weather reporters had to lie to the public about them, saying they were just condensation trails caused by hot air from airplane engines meeting the cold air at thirty-thousand feet. The women wondered why the weather people on the media even felt that they have to explain the strange clouds; evidently people were concerned and wanted to know.

Serena, Jules and Wisdom hoped that people of Verda were finally waking up to what was being done to them. These same self-proclaimed scientist and self-proclaimed medical geniuses had already been successful in dumbing down an unsuspecting human population. They promoted the more affordable, genetically modified organism toxic food to an ever declining in health and over all poorer population. These toxic foods were deliberating created to deplete nutrients from planting soils, and contribute to toxic air and ground water.

These evil reptilian humanoid hybrids roaming the planet of Verda had successfully infiltrated into positions of heads of government and industry, and they were heavily invested in the creation of mandated toxic inoculations, so they stood to gain huge profits. Of course they wanted to keep the program going for as long as possible, so they continued to propagandize and warn the people of the continually mutating variants of the disease that were rapidly spreading across Verda. This program was successful in the way of keeping the inoculations mandated to the citizens; as they wanted everyone to be injected for their huge profits and plans of depopulation. They wanted everyone to get the toxic spike protein into their bodies leading to a slow unsuspecting illnesses and other ever greater threats to the human body, such as strokes, and heart attacks.

They conducted blood drives. Beware and hope those who did want nor have the injections, would have an accident and need a blood transfusion, because the blood will be tainted. It was dystopian and evil on their part. Jules had to agree with Wisdom on that point, and admit it was sinfully genius if you are a monster.

"Deaths would be staggered and look like people died from natural causes and not from a deliberately created disease or from the vicious side effects of the poorly or totally untested, but still permitted for emergency use, toxic inoculations," explained Jules. "This is a case of genocide, and there is no law to stop it because they are all in on it."

The bottom line is that the secret ingredient gain of function deadly bioweapon spike protein eventually would lead to the unsuspecting victim's demise. The depopulation goal was planned by the Verda tyranny globalists, and they are all evil reptilian humanoid hybrids. Jules had to admit that in an evil dangerous sinister way the plan was genius because ordinary citizens of planet Verda were brainwashed to be trusting of their government's oversight committees. It's treasonous, as they all lied to the public, especially the lead country of Malcatraz where the three scientists reside. They had lied and told the humans that all testing proved good, and the injections and strict protocols should be adhered to without exception.

Jules thought that the terrorist like plan was to secretly record and track the habits and activities of the citizens of Malcatraz. This was easily accomplished by sending and receiving certain frequencies to the nano microchips that were implanted in humans through the injections. They were specifically created to not only track, but with gain of function technology, were engineered to eventually control human body functions, thoughts, and activities with a minor variation of frequencies.

Most citizens willingly agreed to stand in line and roll up their sleeves, and received the injections. But Jules' thorough investigating, revealed more and more suspicious negative medical practices were performed that were deliberating killing the people who ended up in the medical facilities. Seems injected victims either shortly died after getting the injections, or they had immediate and horrendous nerve altering side effects that made them shake uncontrollably from head to foot. Many such unsuspecting victims died from strokes, fast growing cancers, and heart attacks. Some could not tolerate the constant shaking all over, with no help or hope for a recovery, so they took their own lives.

Much to their horror, Jules and Wisdom witnessed these atrocities. Patients admitted to medical facilities were abruptly taken off meds they had been on for some length of time. Taken off medicines suddenly can be a shock to the system, thereby, if abruptly stopped, likely would cause strokes and heart attacks. The orders were strictly outlined and monitored, and only certain medicines were permitted to be used. All other normal and beneficial medical treatments and care was to be ignored. Only one procedure monetarily supported by the big drug companies was to be used without exception, or medical workers were to be penalized and ostracized from the medical association.

A ventilator breathing device was to be used in medical clinics. All medical facilities were paid handsomely to follow strict guidelines and procedures, so they readily complied, and they each received a hefty monetary compensation for each device used. The high-pressure ventilators were dangerous to human internal organs and many victims were killed by them. Even so, the well rewarded practice continued as hypnotized and emotionally drained medical workers stood by and watched. If all these medical technicians across the planet of Verda were arrested there would not be enough courts and jails to hold trial. More and more patients who got the mandated injections came down with the debilitating heart and lung conditions which led them to be admitted to medical facilities where they, in a matter of hours, met their demise.

In order to keep their jobs, injections were required. Even if they had previously tested, and the test revealed they had the disease and had natural immunity, they were still required to get the injection.

Jules discovered that was the case ninety percent of the time, the patient was well before they got the injection, only to get the disease after they got the injection. To

Jules, it seemed the real danger was in the injection, not the contagious disease. If a body's immune system was strong and healthy enough, it could easily fight it off. It was as if the proposed dangerous disease seemed to be not as dangerous as the injection that was supposed to protect them.

"The whole thing is a scam," Jules told Wisdom. "It is what the military called a "fifth column" attack. That is, secretly infiltrating the health care system, and buying up the media corporations in order to broadcast their manipulating and brainwashing messages to the public."

"I see what you mean," responded Wisdom, "tell me more." Jules told her all she knew and they both grew ever more suspicious that they were actually experiencing an all-out war on the citizens of Malcatraz and other countries of Verda. The people were reinforced repeatedly by their very own governments through brainwashing techniques.

"This is global war," Jules informed Wisdom.

"We need to call in the Galactic Federation, immediately," offered Wisdom.

People had no clue that they were indeed under an attack by their own corporate backed fascist governments. Jules was convinced this evil conspiracy was planned by the reptilian humanoid hybrid globalist to depopulate Verda was real when she saw that only certain procedures were allowed to be used after the patient's symptoms got so bad that they could no longer draw a breath on their own. Jules began to notice more and more that most patients said that their symptoms did not occur until after they got the injection. The government, which was in cahoots with the medical systems, began mandating most employers mandate injections.

Jules discovered the injections were found to be the real threat; not the said to be contagious disease. So, people were brainwashed, lied to and mentally programmed to believe that the injections were meant to prevent getting the disease; or at least a milder case of it, if they should get it. Major medical alerts were broadcast constantly by the drug corporate owned media, even neighborhood and city centers had Loudspeakers on every corner, demanding everyone get the injection. They warned that the highly contagious deadly disease was spreading at warp speed and that more injections were called for.

The people obeyed and got in line to be injected, again and again. But suddenly more and more deaths were occurring after people got the injections. But people still were not catching on, so more and more people were becoming ill or suddenly dropping dead after getting more of the toxic spike protein injection in them.

Jules secretly had Wisdom forward several injection samples from different areas of Verda to Serena who had them tested and analyzed. The test results revealed toxic ingredients such as polyethylene glycol, aluminum, mercury and fluoride. Ingredients that turned the immune system to high speed and kept it on high speed without a shut off switch. The spike protein was like a runaway high speed rail train stressing the immune system to the point where it eventually turned and attacked the immune system itself. If that did not kill you, it led to more severe illnesses such as autoimmune diseases like lupus, nervous tics, kidney problems, shingles, brain tumors and once dormant, in the state of remission, cancers were returning.

The evil powers that be, headed by three main investors and promoters, the scientist team of Dewy, Cheatem, and Howd, tried to make light of the obvious failure of the injections. It was a fast developed emergency serum, and they stated sufficient testing was done for safety. Being an emergency response injection, it was not yet approved by the government; therefore, the drug companies could not be sued by the injured parties. The drug company backed government stood by the effectiveness of the injections.

To make light of its obvious downfalls, the manufacturers of the inoculations had to say that the intent of the injections was not to stop the disease, but it was designed to make the disease less damaging. Of course, this actually turned out to be false. Many people who were injected either dropped dead shortly thereafter, from anaphylactic shock caused by polyethylene glycol build up in their systems, or the mRNA spike protein that mutates into every organ of the body and nervous system and causes havoc, or the combination of both.

Many persons who had received the injection ended up on permanent disability; which drained government social funds, so everyone's taxes multiplied tenfold. Of course, behind the scenes in secret, the government in cahoots with big drug companies, was offering the medical centers huge monetary rewards and incentives to use only the mandated specific protocols and treatments.

Those who complained of serious side effects like tremors, paralysis, shingles and nervous tics were told they were caused by stress and put on toxic antidepressants. There was no real fix for the horrible side effects. They knew they were caused by the ingredients of the injections. Medical managers knew all along that the terrible side effects, debilitations and sudden death were indeed caused by the injections.

They knew the truth, but the agenda was to depopulate. Orders from high up, by the initial planners such as the reptilian humanoid hybrids team of Dewy, Cheatem and Howd, were to continue issuing lockdown requirements, strict medical procedures, and demand faces be covered with masks. Employees who did not comply were fired and sent prison camp lockups for those who refused to get the injections.

# *Chapter Eleven*

"WISDOM, WE NEED TO WARN the people somehow," ordered Serena after Wisdom updated her and she learned of the deadly situation Jules had been in. Jules managed to escape getting the injection by falsifying records.

"I agree, we need to sneak her out of that medical facility, before they force her to get that lethal injection," confirmed Wisdom. This was the worst case she had ever been on. She began to fear that it was much too big for her to handle alone. This was a case of intended mass murder of the populace by lethal injection.

"This is awful," expressed Serena. "This is worse than the 1940's Earth World War II holocaust of the Jews directed by the German Nazis reptilian humanoid hybrids on that planet. We observed but could not interfere according to universal Galactic Federation law created after we showed ourselves when the they were working on atomic bombs. At that time the Galactic Federation sent several space craft and hovered them over capitol buildings, as a warning. There were photographs of the event. Of course, the photographs were destroyed, and the incident was covered up. It was cases such as that we saw and knew more threats on human life would follow. That was when the Galactic Federation began birthing star seed Pleiadian hybrid humans on Verda--star seed hybrid humans like you two, and me on Verda with special spiritual and telepathic abilities."

"We must stop these insane reptilian humanoid hybrids from committing any further atrocities," exclaimed Wisdom. "They have no moral compass, no conscious, no heart, and no soul. They are pure evil and capable of doing many horrific acts."

******

It was a war on the people and the purpose was to depopulate in a slow unsuspicious way. Deaths would appear as natural deaths, as bodily systems collapse and fail. The majority of the population was highly brainwashed not to see they are being set-up to partake in their own slow demise which is caused by various illnesses brought on by the injections that weaken or totally destroy the human immune system. Since the beginning of the scare tactic program, those who did get the disease and had a rather healthy immune system had no problems in getting well within a few days. But those who got the gain of function spike protein injections as a precaution, were the ones who were hit the hardest. Not by the disease, although it was made to appear so, but rather they were actually taken down by the injection itself, if not physically, then their cognitive skills were hampered.

Only those who were not on prescribed pill drugs, and did not get the injection, were the enlightened ones as they could still think clearly. They were meditating and becoming enlightened and moving out of the third dimensional matrix on up to the fifth dimension of the rest of the universe. Many had been chemical free, as all chemical based medicines were foreign and therefore toxic to the human body. So those who were medicine free, and had tuned out the media frenzy, could see through the forest of propaganda and the vicious lies that were broadcasted by corporate owned media.

The annihilation of the populace was the whole agenda behind the scam of a threat of disease for the purpose to force injections on the people. Depopulation was the war bestowed upon the population of Verda, as the leader of a great reset program was working in partnership with Dewy, Cheatem and Howd. They wanted to depopulate over three quarters of the population and turn the remainder of the population into imprisoned slaves. The remaining population would be put on a government forced program that added a chip in the brain which was connected to a monitoring and control system. The elite running the depopulation program would know everyone's whereabouts at all times, be forced on a government monetary program, and if a purchase or an action was committed that was not approved of, then the person would be fined. Their individual monthly monetary spending allotments would be drastically penalized and reduced.

"Let's be truthful," Wisdom confronted her superior Serena, "people are being viciously attacked by a silent war in the nation of Malcatraz and throughout the whole planet of Verda."

"This is horrible," Serena could not believe a democracy, such as in the country of Malcatraz, would actually deliberately allow a dangerous product to circulate through the lives of their citizens, and use the medical system to mandate an injection that is thought to be toxic. Especially one known to have caused heart failures, sudden deaths, brain tumors, uncontrollable shakes, and left many victims permanently maimed and without any recourse or hopes for a full recovery.

If a victim of constant uncontrollable shaking arrived at a medical facility for help, that person would be met with cold stares by the medical technicians as there was nothing they could do. Oh, they knew what caused the horrible conditions, the injections surely did. But there was nothing they could do. So they told the patients the shakes were the result of depression, and they would hand them a prescription for antidepressants pills, which of course, were made of more of the same toxic chemicals such as the aging factor and brain dulling ingredient, fluoride. In other words, the doctors told the patients their condition was all in their heads.

This finally painted a clear picture for the patients. They were insulted when they realized they had been made a fool of and lied to all along. The medical system had become a toxic dictatorship for their own selfish monetary gain and the destruction of human lives--all part of the new world order great reset and depopulation plan. The people soon realized they were solely on their own in this war against them by their very own leaders. There was no justice, as the whole corporate own fascist government was in on it.

There was no treatment for their horrible injection side effects, the medical advisers merely gave them mood altering psychic meds to shut them up and make them go away. The medical personal were either willingly in on it or were being blackmailed or bribed with huge incentives by big drug companies to participate in the killing and the cover-up. The evil reptilian humanoid hybrids made accomplices of the medical professionals who knew what they was doing was a crime. If all was revealed, they knew they would be the ones who would be the scapegoats, and the leaders at the top, would go free, with millions in their bank accounts.

Doctors knew very well that the injections were the cause of victims' horrific side effects, of which there was no relief or remedies. Once more, the drug companies made sure they had the judicial courts under their control so they could not be touched by lawsuits or arrest. Just like an earlier attack in Malcatraz's largest city called New City, when the reptilian humanoid hybrids rulers blew up buildings killing thousands and blamed the terrorist attack on foreign enemy invaders. In that case, according to Wisdom's investigations, the attack was carried out in order to impose more controlling restraints on Malcatraz's citizens. And most people knew better; but felt powerless.

One new recruit government agent found out about the New City attack and warned her superiors. They shut her up by putting her in a military prison and injected her with mind controlling drugs and shock treatments to erase her memories. Little by little, the government of Malcatraz took more and more freedoms away; innocent groups just meeting together to socialize were forced to disperse. People watched as the installation of spy equipment was positioned throughout cities. Freedom of speech was limited on social media platforms and even meeting in small church groups was forbidden. Everyone was suspect, and the whole New City inside job was just a means to contain and control the people by fear and strip them of more of their freedoms.

That was just the beginning, as they wanted to control what people ate, and not just by eliminating organic foods while forcing toxic genetically modified organisms fake food onto them. No, the drug corporate backed government wanted to end the sale of supplements and force people to have only their chemical drugs to take. A human body needs supplements such as vitamins and minerals.

The only thing they will have left is sunshine. And even with that, the big three scientists Dewy, Cheatem, and Howd, are trying to cover up the sun's rays by spraying chemicals, like aluminum sulfate from airplanes and drones across the sky. Then falsely telling the people, that the thick long streaks of clouds that do not dissipate, are the result of condensation that comes from hot air coming out of the planes' engines and mixing with the cold air at over thirty thousand feet. But true condensation vapor dissipates in minutes, not these chemical filled ones, they hang around and slowly drift changing weather patterns.

Knowing all this made it so obvious that the government of Malcatraz was definitely trying to kill people. There was no nice way to put it, it was that obvious to Wisdom, Jules and Serena. All the star planet members of the Galactic Federation saw it that way too. Verda was indeed a prison planet and apparently now on death row.

Jules saw the government took notice of people taking more and more natural vitamins, minerals and herbs supplements. So the big drug companies running the government were allowed to buy up the supplement companies in order to control their productions and ingredients. People became suspicious and therefore would not buy them anymore, because they felt that they could not trust the government. They witnessed what appeared to be declining health already from the toxic fake non nutritional foods. There were debilitating side effects of pharmaceutical pills and injections, that were media brainwashed on to them by demonic reptilian humanoid hybrids that rose up from the depths of Verda's underground. So far the resistance of the naturalists were holding out and hanging on.

Wisdom went on to tell Serena that those citizens taking natural organic supplements were building up maintaining a healthy immune system and not gotten any signs of having the disease at all. So, of course, the evil powers that be are making it more difficult get their supplements by upping taxes and regulations. It was getting harder to find true organic foods. All the genetically modified organisms that were planted drifted onto other fields from runoff of chemicals sprayed on crops. The soil was bleached and vacant of good healthy minerals. The bottom line, Wisdom realized, was that the humans of Verda were doomed.

"It is a covert attack on the citizens of Verda," explained Wisdom to Serena. "It is a clandestine plan, that when the people get sick enough to be hospitalized, they get roped into more toxins in the way of strict lethal practices. Most humans met their demise in the medical centers. If not, they were moved to nursing centers where the rest of their funds were spent on slow toxic food, pill, and injection way to their demise, drained of all dignity and self-respect by an evil fascist dystopian mindset."

Wisdom went on with her report to Serena, "The government wanted a high death count because of this never ending variant, so called dangerous illness. Actually, the toxic injections and the dangerous hospital procedures, ordered by the drug companies and demanded by the government, were just as lethal if not even more lethal, because no human ever fully recovered. Thus, their depopulation success. In the past few years, deaths had actually decreased in Malcatraz, but more recently with the contagious disease going around and the injection side efforts, mortuaries were reporting that deaths had increased by forty percent. They wanted to see the people filled with worry and fear, as worry and fear wreaks havoc on humans' immune systems."

A plan has been in place for years by the evil fascist government which was bought up and in cahoots with the drug companies. The new world order conspirators wanted to depopulate in a way that makes the deaths look like natural causes. In other words, deaths were blamed on the patient's proposed unhealthy lifestyles. Wisdom and Jules realized that the patients had been set up. The deceased victims were brainwashed by the media commercials that push foods that were sold by taste, certainly not by nutrition. Most of the food pushed for sale in Malcatraz was toxic non-nutritional genetically modified organisms that had been consumed for years and was taking their toll on people's health. Snack foods were addictive and people were becoming obese. When eating nothing but toxic and empty calories without getting the proper nutrition, bodies need to feed the constant craving humans have when they do not get the precious nutrients that they need. Humans are organic as is all of nature; certainly not chemical.

This had been a precursor to the depopulation plan all along and engineered as part of the clandestine plan. The people of Malcatraz and all of Verda, so successfully brainwashed, did not have a clue as they so mistakenly trusted their government's food and drug association's rulings and guidelines. But these genetically modified organism seeds used for planting were injected with toxic herbicides and insecticides. These products were specially designed to be used in most snack products, tasty but non-nutritional treats, and to be used as toxic soybean fake meat products. In other words, people were being either starved to death non-nutritiously or poisoned to death, as more and more natural fruits and vegetables were being modified into toxic products.

For example, Jules proved this to herself when she noticed an apple, she cut in half and put in a container in her refrigerator, and left it there for months--it never turned brown or deteriorated. She noticed to her dismay that it never oxidized and turned brown; like apples normally did. She then remembered she had heard the chemical companies bioengineered apples so they would never get brown. Why, she wondered, was it merely for appearance? She observed the sliced apple she had in the clear container and it appeared only a little dry; that's it, and that was after several months. She thought after that length of time it should have been brown and shriveled. It did not look safe; in fact it looked artificial to her. She remembered why she stuck the apple slices in the refrigerator in the first place. She had tasted it and it had a weird sour taste, like it was bad and rotten, although it looked pretty, fresh, and delicious, which was most puzzling to her.

But not really. She was catching on and becoming more and more aware of the evil ways of the reptilian elitist globalist depopulating ways. She was puzzled, and that was why she kept it to see what would happen to it in time. She threw it out, as she figured that there were chemicals instilled in the creation of that apple. She wished she would have sent it to Serena to run through the lab. The apple had to have been bioengineered. After that heretic experience, she made sure she only bought organic fruit from the local small growers, and she would as long as they are allowed to sell their produce.

The government's war against the people counted on the bad food plan to already have weakened the population's immune system and overall health. So people were set up, and served bad food for poor health in order to weaken their immune systems, to be primed so the falsely proclaimed safe injections would finish them off. The lab engineered bioweapon gain of function, toxic spike protein injections forced the immune system to jump into high speed attack mode. And once on, there was no way to turn it off. Finally the immune system turned on its host.

Jules reported to Wisdom, that besides toxic food, pills, and injections, as if that wasn't blatant enough, another attack was being launched and carried out in full view on the people of planet Verda. Toxic aluminum chemicals were sprayed on them from high flying drones and jet air crafts. She found that more chemicals were being sprayed across the sky intended to block the sun's precious life giving rays and other benefits from reaching the people of Verda. Blocking the sun also threatens the health and lives of plants. For that matter, the sun is the life source of all living things on planet Verda, including humans. Constant low blocked sun light would in time contribute to ill health. All of life on planet Verda needed the sun's rays for growth, and for life to be sustainable. Without the sun, all forms of life dies.

"Wisdom, It is so obvious that the reptilian humanoid hybrids elites are in charge and trying to kill off the human population," warned Jules. "Big business has bought up the government and all the media, so they drenched the public in manipulated fear based propaganda. The daily news, even movies and televised series made declining ill health look like a normal progression of aging and to be expected. The government had recorded all deaths as being contributed to this highly contagious disease, no matter what they really died from. They just wanted to get the numbers up in order to create more fear across the planet, in order to push more injections onto the citizens.

"The purpose of declaring all deaths as caused by a contagious disease was so that mandates would be forced on everyone to be injected. Mandates were enforced to receive even more monetary incentives for medical centers, as the officials in the drug companies were pushing the administration's policies. They knew all too well the food was deliberately being made bad to weaken human immune systems. That set up and primed the way for the injections to be the final punch in the gut, that would push humans, with a weakened immune systems, over the edge into what would be recorded as death by natural causes.

"The medical system was bribed by monetary

incentives, to falsely record the reason for death on death certificates, that the direct cause of death, no matter what they died from, was by the contagious disease out of control all over the planet of Verda. The idea was to keep the threat going so more and more people would be frightened into getting in line and rolling up their sleeves for even more dangerous injections. The plan reaped billions for the drug companies. It was a genius plan.

"First of all the tax payers paid for the various grants that went to the drug companies for research and development. So, the manufacturing of the injections was extremely low cost for them. But the people felt they were not getting what they paid their taxes for in the way of money allocated for the repair of bad roads, failing bridges, and to repair and provide more transit lines. Of course, when they own the government, it's a sure win situation for the drug companies; So people's tax dollars, paid for the development of the toxic injections and then offers them at no charge to the people to rope them in by way of media brainwashing techniques. Genius, and very well thought out, and it all worked very well on a brainwashed preprogrammed populace."

It was very clear to Wisdom and Jules that on planet Verda, people from childhood on up were brainwashed into thinking that they were powerless when it came to their health. "If only they knew," Serena often said, "that our emotions and our minds control our health and aging, if we stay free of pharmaceutical chemicals.

Humans are not made up of chemicals and they are toxic to the human body, causing in time, damage much worse than the ache or pain they were prescribed for. The natural way of getting sun, vibrational, sound, change of diet, lowering stress levels, and eating organic foods to boost the body's immune system. Changing your mind, can change your health."

# *Chapter Twelve*

SERENA REMINDED BOTH WISDOM and Jules that people's minds and their thoughts could determine their overall health and strength of their immune systems. She shared that the practice of fasting, restricted time eating, contributed to having stronger immune systems. Our minds, our conscious or our subconscious thoughts, can even direct our stem cells to go to a certain area of our bodies that need healing and heal it. Our thoughts can even reverse the aging process. Sunshine and grounding oneself can help with that also.

People really are as old as they think they are and want to be, if they do not fall prey to being brainwashed by the corporate owned fascist governments of planet Verda, telling them how long they can expect to live. Men to seventy-six and women until eighty-two seems to be the end game age the government is secretly brain washing people to believe, as people are their thoughts. Older people have most money saved near retirement. So that is when the years of eating bad food can take its toll and seniors enter the medical industry's surgery, treatments, pills and injection trap and then senior living nursing home expenses. It is all designed to get their money; then they can die.

"See," Serena continued, "that is why the powers that be on Verda, do not want people to know just how powerful their minds really are." She told them that is all part of the vicious dangerous scam to mind control and get all citizens to think they are weak and helpless when it comes to their health. That they must have outside help, when the truth is that only people can heal themselves by way of their immune systems; if it's a healthy immune system. Chemicals are useless. In fact they do damage as humans are not chemical. They are not whatever is in the pills or the injections, plus the delivery system agents of polyethylene glycol, mercury, aluminum, or fluoride. Humans are vitamins and minerals and nourished only by organic foods. Just as beef is only as nourishing as the animal's health itself; that is why only organic grass-fed beef is a must.

"We need to somehow get that message out to the citizens," said Wisdom, "I know that seems trivial, but it's all we have to work with."

"I have an idea," pointed out Jules, "We Pleiadians can appear as human or as spirits, right?

"Yes, we can," smiled Wisdom, "how do you think I got here so fast from my beautiful crystal spiral apartment home in Alcyone."

Wisdom loved living on Alcyone of the Pleiades. It was pristine and organic and happy and loving, no one was trying to kill you; like on Verda, where the corporate government is trying to kill its humans off by pitting one against the other, by creating wars, toxic environments and pills and injections. On the Pleiades, there are no conflicts, just love and everyone is very creative, loving, perfectly happy, healthy, young in body, mind and spirit and appear as they wished to be. They lived as long as they want, for what seemed hundreds of years, as there is really no time traced on the Pleiades. And humans of the Pleiades can easily transport in spirit from planet to planet and communicate telepathically just as all passed souls from Verda can.

"So those who passed from the horrendous injection side effects, so tragically, are now in spirit, correct?" asked Jules with a twinkle in her eye and a slight smile on her lips.

"Yes, they are, I see where you are going with this," replied Wisdom.

"Let's engage them in a little tit for tat. What do you think?" asked Jules.

"I think it is our only solution to the problem," said Wisdom.

"I agree," said Jules.

"In spirit form or not, just do not return back to that toxic medical facility," said Wisdom. "There is just too much toxic energy there."

"Don't worry, I will not," confirmed Jules, "I have seen all I needed to see."

And so together they put a plan of revenge of sorts into play. Mind to mind, telepathically, they communicated with all the past souls who either killed themselves or died horrid deaths from side effects after receiving the injections. Wisdom found that all of the passed souls in spirit felt angry for being, wronged, and robbed of their futures. They felt, and rightfully so, that what happened to them was murder. They were angry, and wanted revenge. They knew the evil power forces behind the government had to be stopped, otherwise they would continue with their evil means of depopulating the planet. They felt it was necessary to rid planet Verda of the evil shift changing reptilian humanoid hybrids that silently and secretly invaded, took over, and then led the health care corporations and governments into a secret war on the people by creating toxic air, water, foods, medicines and injections.

The evil reptilian humanoid hybrids' goal was to infiltrate the medical systems with toxic silent warfare. The agenda was aided by brainwashing the populace with continued media broadcasting that sublimely coerced the population into compliancy. Too many people had died from horrific injection side effects, the Pleiadians, leading the Galactic Federation war on the reptiles, were requested to come help by either showing up in space craft or sending a warning to the cabal leaders of the reptilian humanoid hybrids. And by taunting and haunting the three worse reptilian humanoid hybrids that were creating the horrendous mess on Verda, the evil scientist team of Dewy, Cheatem and Howd, along with their team of fascist scientist and government officials. Verda was absent of justice; there was no law in all of Verda to protect the humans.

"Passed soul spirits were the perfect ones to retaliate for justice, as they cannot be seen and can penetrate solid structures such as walls," said Wisdom. "So they are our best solution to ridding Verda of these horrible evil reptilian humanoid hybrids that have infiltrated our societies on Verda for much too long. It's time their rein of the destruction of lives ends."

"I have gathered a large group of passed souls, and they are on their way to personally, in spirit of course, to taunt and haunt Dewy, Cheatem and Howd," reported Jules. "They promise to report back, soon."

# Chapter Thirteen

JULES WANTED TO FOLLOW THE GROUP of souls and observe, but she was contacted by her former coworkers at the medical facilities. Her friend Sally had been held down and forced to get the injection and now she was suffering from serious side effects. Jules rushed right over to see her.

"What do I do, Jules?" cried Sally, "I feel awful. Here I am at home sick in bed and shaking all over. I hope I do not end up like so many others we have seen come into the medical facility."

Jules, being a medical professional, brought with her all the things she thought Sally should begin taking, high potency vitamins and mineral supplements. She brought a grounding sheet for Sally's bed that plugs into the ground portion of an electrical outlet, so Sally could be grounding herself, while getting lots of rest. When she felt a little better, she could get some exercise. Jules would walk with her. They both knew that getting a little exercise would be good for her circulation and help to clear up her lungs. She told her she needed to get lots of sunshine to help build up her immune system. Jules cooked Sally good organic soups and served her healthy fruits and vegetable. She concentrated on giving Sally large doses of vitamin C for an extra immune system boost along with her other important vitamins and minerals. As they both knew that only a healthy immune system can heal a human body.

"I was so stupid," cried Sally feeling horrible. "I should have quite working there like you did. They caught me falsifying my records and knew I lied about getting the injections. They made a mockery of me, and used me as an example. They held me down and jabbed me."

"Since you only had one injection," declared Jules, "I am hoping this regiment of extra vitamins and minerals, grounding yourself by using the grounding sheet, and later on go outside in the sun will help. Walk barefoot in the grass, sit in the sunshine and meditate, concentrate on healing yourself as you meditate, using minds over matter, all that will help."

Jules also reminded Sally to think positive, healing thoughts at all times. Mind over matter is crucial thinking during times of healing as our minds are very powerful. And ask your guides, and passed over love ones to help you heal yourself, and of course, ask our Pleiadian spirit families for help.

Of course, Jules and Sally never learned any of those things in medical training, which was mostly about which pill was used for which ailment, and never really concerned about why a person was not feeling well.

I guess they just weren't that concerned as allopathic technicians rushed between patients every few minutes. So, anything about getting and keeping your immune system healthy had to be learned on your own, for your own personal use, not to discuss with the patient.

Malcatraz drug corporate run government was working on buying up supplement companies; just more evil trickery to rid Verda of humans. They can shut down, or change the formula of supplements, so they do not do a body any good. Because a healthy body is bad for the evil, for profit only, corporate toxic drug business. They would rather have humans on prolonged use of drugs to keep them coming back for more.

Jules had taken it upon herself to research spiritual thinking and mind over matter and self-healing on her own time and shared what she learned with Sally. Our bodies are not chemical. So Jules knew that treating the human body with chemicals will never work. In fact, it will only do more harm, because chemicals are toxic to the human body. Just as toxic injections have done harm.

Jules learned when she read many books written years back that said as much. So she thought, injections may also be a means to distribute nano microchips into unsuspecting people. Because humans are not chemical, but electrical like all in nature is. You are what you eat. So, eating good organic foods is what works to build up and keep a healthy immune system.

In Malcatraz, the Mockeferry Foundation oversaw the

medical training and only taught their students about promoting and pushing chemical pills and injections to the people. Common sense would tell anyone that non organic chemicals are not natural to the human body, and will not work to heal it, but rather work toward fulfilling the real intent, and that is to harm humans. And once the chemical medical system puts humans on pills, they never take them off, it seems, so many times addictions occurred. Humans can only heal themselves through their own immune system, so eating organic and healthily foods is crucial.

When Jules was in training as a spy for the Galactic Federation, she knew the whole Mockeferry method of medical training and their techniques were mainly to train medical personal to push chemical pills and chemical injections. She had done the research, read a lot and learned that most pills and injections were filled with the likes of polyethylene glycol, better known as an ingredient in antifreeze, and a toxic oil derivative.

Jules sent samples to Serena who had pills and injection formulas analyzed, and they reported Jules was correct and that they were also filled with aluminum, fluoride, and mercury. Actually, Jules had been quite appalled upon learning that Verda invested with evil reptilian humanoid hybrids, which have been deliberately poisoning the human population for centuries and continue to get away with it. Reluctantly, but feeling it was necessary, Jules continued with her medical education there in order to gather proof and evidence to be used against them one day, and it appears that maybe that time has now come.

Jules figured that an oil man such as Mockeferry was in it for the huge profits, and since he owned most all the oil refineries wanted in on the deal to get his cut of the profits. Thus, the oil derivative, polyethylene glycol, are in everything from pills, and injections, to pastries baked at food centers across Malcatraz and the rest of Verda.

Jules' research revealed that Mockeferry was a globalist and a member of the illuminati depopulation program gearing up toward a new world order of one ruling regime on Verda. He was in it to see the depopulation new world order being worked out and to satisfy his evil mind set of ridding the population of what he and his fellow evil reptilian humanoid hybrids thought to be lesser-than deserving of living eaters. These evil reptilian humanoid hybrids referred humans as bottom feeders. The goal of the Verda world forum was to deplete Verda of the lesser-than of the population, only keeping a few to be used as slaves on their way to Verda's new world order regime.

For centuries, the evil reptilian race had secretly kept underground where they built cities and roadways deep in the center of the planet of Verda. They ruled and recked havoc on the humans from underground. But after a while, the reptilians wanted to emerge to a surface in their true reptilian form. They wanted to get rid of the humans. So Instead of all-out war attacking humans, they felt it more exciting and genius to steal

DNA from humans and created a male Y chromosome shape shifting reptilian humanoid hybrid to blend in and infiltrate with the human populations on Verda. They were successful in their efforts and the reptilian humanoid hybrids could easily pass and appear as human. Only these reptilian humanoid hybrids had no soul, no conscious, and no emotions other than hate, the will to conquer and destroy, and a driving determination to dominate. They might have looked human on the outside, but they remained just as evil as pure reptiles on the inside.

On the surface of Verda, they easily blended well with humans, all smooth talking and polite. Then, when they had their potential victim in their grip, they turned into psychopaths. They were conniving and cunning, smooth talking, and easily scratched and clawed their way to the top of the heap of social and political status. They headed up large corporations and bought their way into high government positions. The plan was to take over corporations and governments and eventually destroy all the humans on planet Verda, except for a few to be slaves.

And their plan was working as many injected victims fell to horrific side effects that led to death, or the side effects they suffered were so horrific and permanent, many committed suicide to end their misery. Jules had seen this every day at the medical facilities before she quit.

As she visited and cared for Sally, her ill friend, she was so happy to see that her suggestions of a high organic diet of good proteins, lots of nuts, fruits and vegetables, sunshine and grounding was making huge strides in building Sally's immune system to fight off the negative effects that the injection had on her immune system. Sally was happy as well to see that she was slowly getting better.

# *Chapter Fourteen*

ANYONE WITH A HEALTHY IMMUNE system would be fine, but the greedy corporate heads running governments were not pushing good nutrition, healthy sunshine and exercise. Instead, they were pushing their own toxic procedures and products that led to millions of injuries and deaths. Their secret goal was to depopulate on their way to a totalitarian new world order dictatorship with only a few human slaves left to serve them.

Evil was running the whole show as all elite positions were made up of a secret society of the brotherhood of reptilian humanoid hybrids. These evil monsters claimed to own planet Verda. It all began thousands of years ago when the Galactic Federation trapped the evil reptilians underground on planet Verda. The universe could not take any more of their destructive attacks on other planets. So to rein them in, the Galactic Federation placed a satellite moon in Verda's orbit and installed a computer on it. The computer was programmed to hold planet Verda in a third dimensional matrix bubble. The rest of the universe remained in the fifth dimension, as was Verda before it was trapped in a three dimensional matrix to contain the evil reptiles.

In the early days when they arrived on Verda, the reptilians settled in Mu, and most humans lived on Atlan, a neighboring continent, at the time. Armies on Atlan were well equipped with military power, so when the fear mongering reptilians of Mu charged the humans of Atlan, the Atlans had the weapons to fight back and drive the reptilians back underground. The reptilians of Mu were no match for the humans of Atlan, of which many had come from Lyra, and had fought the reptilians there.

When the reptilians from Andromeda attacked Lyra, many humans on Lyra fled, and migrated to the Pleiades and to Atlan. The Atlans were victorious and forced the evil reptilians of Mu underground during the chaotic battles that followed.

Eventually, the reptilians learned how to hack the computer on Verda's moon and gave themselves knowledge to steal DNA from the humans, creating the male Y chromosome reptilian humanoid hybrid. The reptiles were successful is creating reptilian humanoid hybrids that could easily shift change from looking reptilian to looking fully human. They wanted to appear human so that they could easily mix and mingle with the humans living on the surface of Verda. It all began, when the reptilians had to be contained, and the Galactic Federation's idea was to contain them somewhere before their vicious attacks of blowing up and destroying planets would throw the whole balance of the galaxy out of whack.

Having landed on Verda, the reptilians claimed Verda as their own. They went underground there to hide from the humans living on the surface of Verda. But the reptilians were smart and determined not to go down easily. They found ways to hack the computer on Verda's moon, and gave themselves more power over the humans. They thought, why create wars and use weapons when they could infiltrate Verda's surface as human like reptilian humanoid hybrids and be able to mingle with the humans.

As reptilian humanoid hybrids they easily blended in with Verda's human societies. But reptilian humanoid hybrids remained evil. Humans had a heart, soul, feelings, and a conscience, which certainly did not carry over in the DNA that the reptilians stole from the humans in order to become reptilian humanoid hybrids. The reptilian humanoid hybrids were extremely vicious and soon discovered their taste for young human flesh and blood, thereby creating deadly satanic rituals. They infiltrated all heads of religious sects and created secret demonic rituals, involved pedophilia, sex slaves, and were just pure evil satanic rituals.

The plan was to shift change from reptilian to reptilian humanoid hybrids, until they could rid Verda of most of the humans, build up enough resources to rise up, and then to expose their true reptilian appearing selves. They would do this after conquering and ridding Verda of most of the nasty humans and turn the remainder of them into slaves.

The evil reptilian humanoid hybrids figured the best way to manipulate and control humans was to infiltrate the medical systems of Verda, and create a disease; and then created a toxic injection claimed had to be used against that disease. Only the disease was not as deadly as the proposed fix, the required injections. So if the disease did not kill off humans, then the injections would eventually. The injections were filled with toxic ingredients such as polyethylene glycol an oil product that was one of the ingredients used in antifreeze, which Jules had discovered to her horror. Also used was mercury, aluminum, fluoride and others. The combination of toxic ingredients, caused blood clots and other problems that appeared as natural declining health toward a slow death; but medical workers saw far too many cases arising soon after humans got their injections.

Suddenly mortuaries reported a forty-percent increase in deaths, as many humans suffered sudden heart failure and dropped dead during daily activities such as while driving motor vehicles, passing out, or dying, and crashing them. Seeing this many deaths and catching on to the evil tactics of the for-profit medical systems, many medical workers made up a new word and became calling the large increase of accidents, "Vaccidents."

It was unfathomable to the population to even think that their very own government of Malcatraz, could be so cruel; But that was how they got away with it. Normal people could not fathom that a government would do that to their very own citizens. And that was how and why the citizens were subtly brainwashed through media news and other programs. But like Jules, some people were spiritually tuned into their intuition and were wise to doubt the government's free injection programs for various reasons.

Number one, the medical system was a for-profit system; everyone knew that. Number Two, why, if the government was so concerned about everyone's health, did they not stop the growing and distribution of toxic genetically modified organisms for food? And number three, why did they not insist that people take vitamins and mineral supplements in order to build up their immune systems to be able to fight off the disease?

Instead the food and drug association of the Malcatraz's government silenced these practical suggestions. A good immune system was all that was needed to ward off this disease that was claimed to be so very contagious. I would be very mild if everyone had a good healthy immune system to fight it off. And once they got a mild case of the disease, the people would have an antibodies against it, and typically not get it again.

But those ideals ran contrary to the evil reptilian humanoid hybrid cabal's plan. They thought that there were just too many nasty humans roaming their planet, Verda, that the reptilians claimed and wanted all to themselves. It's not that the populace had gained trust of the for-profit medical system. It's more that most of the people were media brain washed at the onset starting many years ago. Televised messages suggested that if you had certain symptoms to tell your medical personnel about a certain drug you wanted to take for it, thus mental programming. And the medical system media messages also made it clear that people only lived to a certain age; an age they suggested.

All was for the purpose of mind programming; that occurred so sly and slick that people did not even know that it was happening. And then you get families and friends together, and being all of the same media mindset; reinforce each other's beliefs. But if people would have only thought about it, they would have seen the toxic ways of the food and drug system. First, control human thoughts, then push genetically modified organism of fake foods to poison and weaken their immune system. Tell people the sun is bad for you only to suggest skin protecting products that actually, when mixed with the heat of the sun, sparked skin cancers. All good clues that the reptilian humanoid hybrids were only out to destroy the human population.

Jules shared with her Galactic Federation team what she had learned. She told them, "If it seemed people were not succumbing, and falling ill fast enough from the threatening contagious disease, then they mandated that all the people be injected. And with the final punch in the gut, be injected with a lethal injection chemical attack! Humans are not chemical; humans are electrical, like all of nature; and humans need vitamins, minerals, and organic foods; human are one with the universe. The evil reptilian humanoid hybrids real secret clandestine plan of attack was to depopulate by the toxic injections. That is why injections were mandated."

Jules discovered that was the plan from the beginning of the project. Jules had been suspicious all along of the for-profit medical systems of Malcatraz and the other nations of Verda. She had suspected all along they were up to no good especially after she heard plans about a new world order of one government for the whole planet of Verda. Malcatraz was to catch up with the already other totalitarian nations of Verda, and entrap the humans into slavery and servitude. Jules could not believe that a nation would deliberately clandestinely attack its own people; but nations have gone to war to protect their for-profit interest, so evidently human life meant nothing to these vicious reptilian humanoid hybrids.

The injections were deliberately made toxic to destroy the bodies' immune system so it would turn on itself. But as Jules and Wisdom and their fellow Pleiadians of the Galactic Federation soon discovered, the evil depopulation scheme was actually still in progress. They were not letting up and there was no one to stop them. There was no oversight or court of law to stop what was going on, because all law officials were bought and paid for by the evil reptilian humanoid hybrids in high places. They were either bought off, tricked or blackmailed into carrying out strict orders on how to treat patients.

It was all controlled by an ag-old illuminati group of evil reptilian humanoid hybrids, call the cabal or called the shinning ones. All humans on Verda were doomed, period, end of story, unless, Serena and her team from the Galactic Federation could somehow stop them. Jules was still waiting to hear back from the passed souls soccer players who were planning on taunting and haunting the disease creating evil ring leaders Dewy, Cheatem and Howd.

The Pleiadians knew of the evil plans by Dewy, Cheatem and Howd as they had been monitoring them for years. A full out attack by the Galactic Federation on Verda was too dangerous for the humans, so they had birthed their own Pleiadian human hybrid star people on Verda to monitor and report the doings of the shape shifting reptilian humanoid hybrids' murderous plans. Indeed, they were on Verda to try to warn people, but the humans on Verda were too easily brainwashed and mind controlled from birth.

They took on their parents' beliefs, then they were religiously brought up and taught in schools to honor and obey the authorities of church and government, so they were all set up to believe and trust the medical systems. The depopulation through illness plan began years back when the medical systems developed the hypodermic needles. Soon diseases were created. Then they began promoting injections for newborns as protection against possible future fictitious ailments.

Humans were warned against threats of horrific diseases and deadly influenzas, so they were easily persuaded by medical personal to be injected against them. As more and more injections of various sorts were injected, more babies became autistic, a brain dulling side effects of the injections. Brainwashed parents did not see the dangers and of course were taught and programmed to listen and obey authority figures. Even if parents were concerned, they still went ahead as their friends and neighbors did, and got the children injected in order for them to enter the education systems in the nation of Malcatraz. It was the law, all youths must be injected to get an education.

The people were well raised and conditioned to obey authority figures and too brainwashed to catch on to what was really going on. As they were taught from little on up to listen and obey persons of authority. Of course, along the way, the people were chipped too, as the nano microchips were conveniently hidden in the injection serum. These injected nano microchips could easily be programmed by controlled frequencies. Vibrations were sent through the air waves to adjust just how docile and obedient they wanted the humans' brain to be. If they monitored someone getting too uppity and frisky, they merely zapped them back into a docile state. If there was an uprising and questioning of the government's rules or of the medical system, they were zapped. The mad scientist team of Dewy, Cheatem and Howd, could remotely send out frequencies to a specific targeted area to calm down the mischievous revel-rousers. Their goal was to have every human on Verda chipped for mind control and gain of function of their immune systems.

Wisdom and her team of researchers received samples of the serum Jules had taken from the medical facility before she resigned. Upon examining them, they did indeed discover implanted nano particle microchips in the injection serums. These nano particles microchips would allow humans to be easily brainwashed into docile and obedience citizens just by merely sending out a certain frequency that the nano particle microchips picked up. The evil reptilian humanoid hybrids in power, found that they could easily influence human behavior. When Wisdom learned about this, she pleaded with Serena to send in the Galactic Federation's troops to end this madness.

"Well, right now, since the reptiles on the surface of Verda are shape shifted into reptilian humanoid hybrids and disguised as humans, we can not that easily pick out the evil humans from other humans," explained Serena. "We are working fast on computerized facial recognition technolog. Then we'll go after them, one by one."

"I just hope it is not too late, then," worried Wisdom.

"Me too," echoed Jules.

"Can't the Galactic Federation just vaporize Dewy, Cheatem and Howd?"

"We have to be discreet," answered Serena, "Galactic rules."

"Rules, rules," Jules responded with disgust.

No space craft was needed as more of the Galactic

Federation's members of Pleiadian humans were teleported in spirit form from the Pleiades to planet Verda. They arrived on planet Verda in seconds and then easily transformed back into human beings. They arrived in order to infiltrate the populations and investigate. Any messages delivered to the humans had to be by way of secret telepathic means to be intercepted by the spy Pleiadians, as the reptilian humanoid hybrids censored all media outlets.

The human star seed hybrids from the Pleiades who were on Verda were intuitive and psychic and well connected to the spirit world on the other side. So they received messages telepathically warning them of what was to come. The most recent message was a warning that another round of injections was to be mandated. Jules, of the Pleiades and a member of the Galactic Federation, was warned not to participate in any medical programs that were coming up, and to turn off any media broadcasting programs. She tried to convince her partner Sally and others to also do the same.

Sally was feeling better and slowly getting back to good health. It was crucial now as the evil reptilian humanoid hybrids had upped the game with another round of even more toxic injections to be forced onto the humans of Verda. Slowly but surely, Sally was doing much better and nearly back to her normal healthy self. The natural healing way was working. Jules made sure that Sally only ate organic foods and knew to stay away from taking any over the counter remedies sold in food centers as they all contained about the same toxic brain dulling ingredients as the injections: aluminum, mercury, and polyethylene glycol an antifreeze ingredient.

Jules suggested Sally meditate or read something while sitting outdoors in the sun, instead of staying inside and watching the dangerous brainwashing programs on the broadcasting tube. Jules had learned that the team of Dewy, Cheatem, and Howd were very crafty in sending out subtle messages via news programs. Even children's programs were created to be mind controlling using certain words to trigger a trance in the human brain.

Wisdom and Jules tried to warn others that the media was being used to brainwash people into believing and fearing a highly contagious lethal disease was spreading across the planet of Verda. Nevertheless, the population was told not to worry, that a gain of function spike protein injection was fast being distributing and becoming available soon to all areas. It will attack and conquer the vicious disease or at least make it less dangerous and keep citizens out of the medical facilities, and from dying. What the population did not know, however, was that the gain of function ingredients in the injections were not for diminishing the effects of the disease. But were intended to diminish the function of the human brain and the immune system and therefore eventually resulting in death appearing as death by natural causes. The plan was to promote a series of injections to ensure the gain of function of the human immune system and take it down.

All media broadcasting personnel and programs were used to propagandize and brainwash an entire population into receiving the series of injections. The new world order globalist leaders of all the countries of Verda eagerly suggested that everyone get them. They were all in on it.

The head of the country of Malcatraz mandated these injections starting in the areas he thought to be the most undesirable minority groups, women, non-whites, and the poor. It was the evil reptilian humanoid hybrids running the government that created race decision and poverty to make beggars and pleaders of them. just so the self-serving reptilian humanoid hybrids ruling gods could choose who received the better benefits. They created the lesser-than groups, to build their own patriarchal egotistical, narcissistic superior mind sets. They actually thought the common people were too naive to see through their evil self-serving tactics, and therefore could easily convince the people to get the injections.

To set the example, they broadcasted members of government getting the injections, but actually they only pretended to get the injections. It was just a publicity stunt by the reptilian humanoid hybrids in positions of power. They knew for sure that the citizens of Verda would soon be totally programmed and frightened into compliancy.

But some humans working in the medical professions had been paying attention and grouped together to break away and secretly start up their own natural holistic healing centers in order to work with those victims who received injection injuries.

# *Chapter Fifteen*

"YES, SOME HUMANS HAVE BEEN paying attention and heard the words put out by the resistance groups of medical workers, who would rather quit the evil medical system than be part of what they thought was an obvious murderous plot produced by their very own corporate controlled fascist government. The resistance teams quit and struck out on their own and started their own natural health recovery programs to aid the injection victims and to speak out against receiving the injections in the first place. They thought people should quit their jobs rather than be forced to get the injections. They vowed to help the victims of side effects injuries who had already fallen prey to the noxious injections," noted Wisdom. "We have warned many ahead of time through seminars and other means, that news shows should not be monitored, and the broadcasting tubes should be kept off, as brainwashing by the media was a large part of the outreach mind programming plan."

"It's fortunate that many are becoming more suspicious," said Wisdom, "and refused the mandated injections, even if it meant losing their livelihood positions over it."

"Yes, many citizens of the nation of Malcatraz, where Wisdom and her team of Pleiadian star seed hybrids were sent, for the very purpose of one day warning the people of the coming atrocities of the corporate government partnership that is ran by the evil reptilian humanoid hybrids who are slaves of the Illuminati. It was thought that the medical and government news propaganda be dissected and taken seriously, for they, the medical and corporate backed government, had already been pushing toxic non-nutritional genetically modified organisms of grains and seeds onto the public," explained Wisdom, "along with pills that have serious toxic side effects to the immune system." So bad meds, bad foods, and now the citizens were supposed to trust the news media and the pushy government propaganda rhetoric of which the sole purpose was to brainwash and manipulate citizens into willingly roll up their sleeves and patriotically and proudly receive their mandated injections multiple injections whenever they came out with a threat of a new disease variant.

Citizens were so brainwashed and manipulated as to brag as though it was a badge of honor to roll up their sleeves and get their infections. They proudly went sleeveless to sport colorful Band-Aids over the injection prick sites to show the world they were obedient to their almighty fuehrer team of Dewy, Cheatem and Howd. The injections of course were mandated, in order to keep social privileges and it meant the difference between keeping or losing your job, being able or not able to fly on passenger planes, being able to buy food at food centers, or being able to purchase petroleum to run their vehicles.

The planet of Verda, out of greed of a few, was still running vehicles on petroleum. Whereas other planets in the galaxy were for more advanced, using the ancient extraterrestrial installed pyramids for total free electricity. Verda had the ancient pyramids situated around the planet, but greedy oil producing tyrant reptilian humanoid hybrids such as Mockeferry Foundation hid the free energy spots in order to charge the public and make himself extremely wealthy. Verda's technology was far behind the rest of the planets in the universe, and no other planets were using backwards and antiquated petroleum products. They were using crystal based pyramid producing free electrical energy. Their vehicles were both clean and natural based on zero-point anti-gravity technology.

Because of the greed of the reptilian humanoid hybrids raising to the top of Verda's economy, Mockeferry Corporation and Foundation kept technology stalemated using antiquated petroleum in vehicles and spewing out toxic exhaust that chocked the atmosphere of Verda, and contributed to deadly unhealthy air--all out of greed of one selfish, evil, reptilian humanoid hybrid.

Serena and her team of Pleiadians were positioned on planet Verda to enlighten the humans there and explain to them how they have been the subjects of pure greed and evil for centuries. They explained that the lower vibrations of the third dimensional bubble surrounding Verda, and entrapping the reptilians there, was slowly fading and that the evil reptilians could not survive out of the lower vibrations of the third dimensional matrix, so they would perish in a cloud of dust.

Then all humans will be free to realize their own mind's spiritual potential and powers, and that all humans are spiritual beings on Verda living as human beings. They have the power to heal themselves and others, via mind-to-mind loving thoughts and meditations. They will be free from the horrible atrocities bestowed on them by the evil ones. When the third dimensional veil is lifted, they will all be free to easily communicate with their passed loved ones in spirit, as spirit souls are energy, and energy never dies. Unlike the evil soulless reptilians that will perish when the lower vibrations of the third dimensional matrix is dissolved and Verda rejoins the rest of the universe that is in the higher vibrations of the fifth dimension. In the fifth dimension, human bodies will become lighter, are more crystal like, more telepathic, and will be able to transport the universe and visit other planets in spirit form, much like Serena, Wisdom, Jules and others from the Pleiades can already do, as can the whole of the universe that is already in the fifth dimension.

Being an evil reptilian humanoid hybrid, Mockeferry's view, was that greedy profits gained were more important than being futuristic and saving lives of the people and the planet. In fact, just the opposite was true. Mockeferry insisted his petroleum products be used in all prescribed and over the counter medicines that can be purchased without a prescription from a medical technician. Pills and injections were pushed onto the public, although they had no health benefits. Quite the contrary, they were very toxic to the human brain and body. Still, Mockeferry bought his way into the government's oversight committee and insisted polyethylene glycol, a type of oil product used as antifreeze, be added to all medicines, injections, and food, such as bakery products.

Mockeferry had the market on petroleum, and it was the only product permitted to be used in the powering of all vehicles on planet Verda. All companies that had the audacity to rise up, develop and produce electric, anti-gravity, or other types of energy powered vehicles, were quickly sabotaged or bought up only for the purpose of shutting them down and put out of business. As all it was done as a way to discourage anyone else from even thinking of trying to do the same. Greedy, just one evil reptilian humanoid hybrid, Mockeferry, personally kept Verda in the energy stone age out of pure selfish greed in order to build his own power and wealth and to dominate and control the whole planet of Verda.

So Verda, especially, the nation of Malcatraz was already under a vicious totalitarian rule, falsely claimed as a two party democratic republic. Mockeferry, a greedy, egotistical, narcissistic reptilian humanoid hybrid, considered himself a god above all others, and of course he wanted his profit share in the depopulation plan. So he contributed to it and got his cut of the revenues by insisting polyethylene glycol, had to be added and used in everything. It's all about his greedy huge profits, certainly not about the lives of the people of Malcatraz or of the rest of planet of Verda as his widely distributed toxic products dominated the global markets.

Wisdom's team of chemist investigators easily found Mockeferry's toxic products everywhere, in bodacious fashion, proudly listing aluminum and polyethylene glycol ingredients on labels as part of the ingredients. Why not? Brainwashed people had not the wit about them to even question an ingredient and its use, because they were mentally programmed and conditioned to obey all powerful patriarchal authoritarian figures.

But there was a few, those connected spiritually with their guides and souls of passed loved ones on the other side of the veil, who were intuitive and psychic, exchanging mind to mind messages. As humans are spiritual beings in human form with consciousness, our souls and minds are energy and never die, and our minds are all connected. And many humans who saw the atrocities of what was happening on Verda, were waking up to that, as they were already living in the reality of the higher fifth dimension. More and more were learning and were catching on to the evil ways of what was going on. Slowly but surely, the humans on Verda took the time to follow the money chain and learn by listening to and reading many articles by the members of the resistance groups that were popping up everywhere on certain sites.

These groups were mainly begun by disgruntled medical professionals who refused to continue to be a part of the toxic chemical medical systems war on the citizens of Verda. And if anyone really thought about it, they realized that humans are not chemical; they are electrical as the whole of nature is electrical on Verda and of the universe. Chemical treatments merely add insult to injury and cannot heal nor sustain life, rather over time, chemicals only make conditions more deadly. And once more, usually caused the ill conditions by way of bad foods in the first place, so further chemical treatments will slowly in time merely cause a person to succumb to toxic chemical side effects.

Secret articles distributed by the resistance groups explained as much, and were published and circulated out of the main stream, and easily found, if people wanted to resist the state of denial and learn the truth--that their very own vicious evil reptilian humanoid hybrid ran government was trying to kill them off. The truth was hard to face. The fact that you had been had by religions, and corporate backed governments, that are run by evil reptilians humanoid hybrids, that you were imprisoned on Verda while in the low vibrations of the third dimension.

The universal Galactic Federation entrapped humans there with them on Verda. They felt they had to stop the evil reptilians from destroying other planets in the universe. At the same time they also tried to enlighten the humans how to save themselves and rise above the evil. But most people became aware out of sheer common sense by seeing who had the most to gain. People began to easily see that the ways of the powerful were evil and destructive for the people of planet Verda. The authors of truths knew the leaders of their corporate backed fascist governments were up to something, and that something was not good.

Serena explained all this to the team and more. "We need to warn more of the citizens of Malcatraz and the rest of planet Verda, that is, if it is not too late," insisted Serena with urgency in her voice

"It might be too late, I'm afraid," warned Wisdom. "Those who got the injections received the toxic gain of function mutating spike protein along with the other toxic ingredients, that attacks the blood system and organs. Serena, the real threat is not the proposed dangerous disease, which was a scam to quickly get an emergency injection developed and jabbed into the people out of claims that it was the only defense available for that particular disease. The plan was that by using government persuading techniques, such as mind control and brainwashing, millions would receive the mandated injections and then would eventually die from it. But they would record the deaths as deaths by natural causes, certainly not death caused by the toxic ingredients in pill and injections that were mandated on the human victims."

"It is nothing but a well-planned clandestine all-out war on the citizens of Verda!" exclaimed Serena.

"Yes, it is a war on the humans of Verda," agreed Wisdom. "It's an all-out covert attack to depopulate Verda, so the reptilians in their pure reptilian form can surface and come out from underground and live on the surface of Verda as the true reptilians beings they are. They would no longer needing to shift change into reptilian humanoid hybrids disguised to appear human."

"That is so alarming," cried Serena.

"Oh, but wait," Wisdom said with hope in her voice. "I just got word from our Galactic Federation's commanding crew stationed on Verda's moon monitoring the third dimension computer that they have found a way to reverse the programs. The evil reptilians hacked the computer and manipulated it to send frequencies to give the reptilian humanoid hybrids the power to shift change. They wish to lower the frequency. In fact, they are looking into ways to totally shut off the computer on the moon permanently, ending the third dimensional matrix, and restoring Verda to the universal fifth dimension with the rest of the universe. No longer will it be in its own unique prison of a third dimensional matrix bubble."

"What will happen then?" asked Serena.

"Well once the computer on the moon of Verda is shut down, Verda's evil third dimensional matrix will end and Verda will return to the fifth dimension to match the fifth dimension of the rest of the universe," explained Wisdom.

"And what will happen to the reptilian human hybrids and the citizens of Verda?" asked Serena.

"Well, the reptilians can only survive in the third dimension, so they will no longer be a threat as they will merely self-destruct into a dusty wisp of a dark clouds and disappear off planet Verda, to disperse out into the ether and dissolve into nothingness. The reptiles cannot survive in the eighty percent oxygen, twenty percent nitrogen crystal lined destiny of the fifth dimension, as they could in the third dimension of the matrix which was just the opposite: twenty percent oxygen and eight percent nitrogen," explained Wisdom.

"Now, it's a race, for the Galactic Federation team on the moon of Verda to get the computer reprogrammed or shut down before the evil, crafty, reptilians humanoid hybrids, do more damage to all life on Verda and end up killing everyone off," explained Serena.

Serena reminded her team of Pleiadians star seeds on Verda that they needed to get the word out that the human mind is very powerful and can heal itself and reverse diseases. It is the one most important things that the vicious reptilian humanoid hybrids wanted to hide and cover up. And they were successful through mind controlling religious teachings.

They made humans believe they were powerless in mind, body and spirit as a means to enslave them. Serena's team was determined to have humans on Verda learn that their minds are very powerful, and their thoughts control their health, wellbeing and their realities.

The resistance teams on Verda were conducting meetings and teaching humans that it was possible to reconnect with nature by meditating to change your mind, change your thoughts, change your body, and improve your heath. Humans on Verda were becoming more enlightened spiritually as the third dimensional veil was lifting. People were becoming more mindful of their emotions and releasing negative stressful thoughts that had the potential to cause havoc on their immune systems and allow disease to form. Negative thoughts can be reversed, into loving thought processes and can reverse ill health conditions and heal the body.

The reptilian humanoid hybrids powers that be, do not want humans to know that, nor just how powerful and self-healing human minds and thoughts are. Mind controlling techniques used by vicious religious sects helped to destroy this knowledge, brainwashing humans into thinking that they were weak and helpless and needed outside help. They were brainwashed to believe they were born as evil sinners and not to trust themselves and their own intuitions. Anyone found out to have a spiritual mind or thought was branded an evil witch. They were immediately socially ostracized and committed to mental facilities, locked away and injected with dangerous toxic drugs to silence them. That was what life in an evil third dimensional medical and mental prison run by Mockeferry was like in the nation of Malcatraz and the rest of Verda.

The Mockeferrys ran a fear based health care system, and the plan was to keep humans in fear and worry in order to weaken their immune systems. Thus, the fighting two party system that pretended to be a democratic republic was no such thing, and all election outcomes were predetermined by the cabal of the Illuminati. This practice was throughout the whole planet of Verda. The corporate run government warned of a possible pending new world order agenda consisting of one world leader dictatorship.

But the truth was, it was already a dictatorship, using fear mongering to control the human population. For fear was the strong driving force in mind control on their road to depopulation. The plan was to provide only toxic genetically modified organisms in the food supplies which were toxic to the human immune systems. The whole idea was humans would get sick and be put on for-profit long term medicinal and injection regiments, never to be taken off, until they eventually succumbed to the chemical toxins and died.

Verda had become a prison planet for all humans as the team of vicious reptilian humanoid hybrids of Dewy, Cheatem, and Howd had scratched and clawed their way to the top positions until they rose to total power. They ran the food and drug associations allowing only toxic genetically modified organisms, without nutritional value, to be sold as food. They bought all the good farmland so no one else could own it. They eliminated grass fed animal food products and humans were forced to eat only engineered genetically modified organisms that were non-nutritional foods. All plants grown were non-budding nor reproductive as they were the toxic genetically modified organism type plants. All of this, topped with applied fear and stressful situations would soon lead all humans to ill health and their demise.

The humans of Verda's one government rule had failing immune systems leading to the total demise of humans on planet Verda. The reptilian humanoid hybrids planned it this way, as they wanted the humans on Verda to have nothing but unhealthy things to eat. It was all done so their immune systems would be weakened and therefore get hit drastically by the threat of a major contagious disease, that would cripple all of Verda's social and economic status. But the reptilian humanoid hybrids running the government promised a life-saving emergency injection was on the way and soon to be available without cost to all of Verda.

All medical facilities throughout the nation of Malcatraz and other nations on Verda were gearing up to be prepared, and Jules, a star seed from the Pleiades, assigned to Verda to work in a medical facility and reported back to the Galactic Federation her findings.

# *Chapter Sixteen*

JULES, A TOP RANKED MEMBER of Wisdom's spy team, was a Pleiadian star seed. Her soul and spiritual being originated from the Pleiades Seven Sister Star System ruled by women. Although her soul was birthed on Verda, she could easily teleport in spirit form back and forth from planet Verda to her crystal terrace and spiraling high rise apartment on Alcyone, the brightest and central star, of the Pleiades.

She preferred to work from her home monitoring activities logged into Verda's moon computer which controlled the third dimension matrix surrounding planet Verda. But on occasion, such as this, her team leader and commander, Wisdom, had her teleport to Verda on a spy mission in Malcatraz. There, Jules was stationed as a scientist in a huge medical facility. This was her undercover assignment, and strategically front line position, where she was to observe and listen in order to gather information. Wisdom wanted boots on the ground, so to speak, as dangerous actives there were heating up on planet Verda. Another round of toxic injections was being mandated by the drug corporate owned government.

Wisdom had positioned Jules there as she had reports that a particular medical facility had the largest treatment center and heaviest distribution of the injections. The injections were mandated because the government said they would prevent or weaken the effects of the contagious rare disease that was circulating and would be one of the main distribution centers for the injections.

Corporate owned media ran specific programs that brainwashed citizens so they happily and willingly stood in line for hours, to get the injections. They readily obeyed. Loudspeakers tragically placed around the cities shouted out government's warnings that the disease would surely kill them, if they did not get the injections. Those, who questioned, hesitated or who refused to get them were rounded up, labeled treasonous, and locked up in prison camps until they caved and received the injections. Some people are just harder to brainwash than others.

The injections were free and at no cost to the citizens because of the good will of the government, which left a few to question why a normally for-profit medical system would suddenly be so generous and care about the people. Just what were their motives? Jules wondered. After all, if they were so worried about people's health and welfare she wondered, why did the government allow toxic genetically modified organisms to even be called food, much less actually be used as food and not rodent kill? The food, that the government certified as safe, and pushed onto the people, was actually made with toxic organisms that depleted the immune system's ability to maintain good health. That was the question Jules pondered as she saw sick people come into the medical facility.

Most of the people she discovered got the disease after they got the injection. Because of their drugged up foggy thinking, they never put two and two together, as Jules did. She saw that most people got ill after they got the injection and not before. So, she determined that it was indeed the injections that were wreaking havoc on people's immune system. The injections were attacking the health of the human body rather than saving it. The drug corporation controlled fascist government, with repeated orders through the controlled media, demanded the people get the injection; as the injections were the only way to escape sure death from the very dangerous, and very rare disease that remained without a name or place of origin.

"Wisdom, they are deliberately maiming and murdering people. If I baked a cake injected with toxic polyethylene glycol and gave it to my neighbor, and she ate it and died, and the law had an autopsy performed and it was known that I gave her the cake. I would be arrested and sent to prison for murder," complained Jules. "But these vicious, pretend to be human, reptilian humanoid hybrids, are able to get away with murder."

"I know, and I agree," sympathized Wisdom. "They get away with it because everyone is in on it willingly, or has been blackmailed or tricked into partaking in satanic pedophile sacrifice rituals; therefore, forced to comply or have their lives and careers ruined."

"And again, of course, with this latest round of injections, a very large number of people who were recently injected are showing up at the medical facilities with complaints of experiencing various side effects. Many of the victims are experiencing uncontrollable and violent head, body and extremities shaking and twitching. Some have violent and uncontrollable facial tics, burning and itching rashes, and over all outer epidermis and inner dermis burning sensations. Seems the injection ill effects were mostly centered in the human nervous system. Many patients were complaining of uncontrollable shaking legs, making it impossible to walk, much less stand in place. Some complained that the itching rashes and nervous twitching tics were driving them crazy. It also appeared that their pre-conditions worsened after receiving each additional mandated injection.

Jules was curious to hear what her supervisor of the medical facility had to say. So she had mentioned what she was seeing to the floor administrator. Just as she had predicted, he blew her off and more or less ignored her concern, casually claiming those various side effects were just due to the patient's stress and ordered her and her co-workers to send those people back home with prescriptions for anti-depressants. Of course Jules knew, but most medical facilitators had no clue those anti-depressant prescriptions were loaded with polyethylene glycol and aluminum--just more of the same stuff that was in the injections.

So the victims were merely adding insult to injury that would eventually lead to their untimely demise. It was an act of homicide, but as planned, deaths would be recorded as a death due to natural causes. Jules reported this information back to her team leader, Wisdom. Wisdom in turn, reported the information back to her commander, Serena. Needless to say, they were appalled, and realized the criminality of the situation. The problem was, it appeared that all of the department of justice was blackmailed to turn a blind eye, as was the rest of the corporate owned government. They would have to call in the troops on this one, and that meant demanding the Galactic Federation shut down the computer on Verda's moon, to end the third dimension matrix that Verda was trapped in.

Jules was working in the medical clinics. She experienced more and more inoculated people coming to the clinic with various and strange symptoms. Her superior ordered her to send them home with yet another noxious solution, a lethal prescription, as there was only one certain strict protocol for medical workers to follow. They were threatened by fear of dismissal, if they swayed from it. Patients returning soon after getting the injections, who the clinic personal thought were not yet sick enough were actually sent back home and told to return back to the clinic only when their symptoms became worse. Of course their symptoms got worse, much worse, until they could barely breath.

And when those people came back to the clinic, the medical technicians were required to follow the strict regimen of health care procedures that were outlined in their instruction manuals.

The first thing was to put them on a ventilator machine that forced high pressured oxygen down their throats; This was strictly followed as the medical facilities received handsome monetary kickbacks for each ventilator used. But the ventilators were dangerous, the forced oxygen pressure was too much for the patient to bare, and the harsh and dangerous ventilator treatments were so invasive and brutal that most patients died during the procedures. But the medical facilities still got their monetary reward for using a ventilator. Ventilators were used because they brought one of the biggest bonus paybacks to the facility, and so the more they used them, the bigger the medical facilities financial accounts grew. But only after a good amount was directly transferred into the facilities administers' private bank accounts.

Jules, kept her head down, and worked diligently as she listened and over heard some very interesting conversations among the various administrators. She had come to the conclusion that evil reptilian humanoid hybrid crooks were everywhere and permeated all of Malcatraz's medical systems. They were everywhere.

The practice of bribe and reward continued on, and each medical facility received bonuses from the government for following the government's contagious disease department's strict orders. With further investigation, Jules learned why the clinic handled sick people the way they did. It was because the government was giving monetary incentives for each breathing device that was used, and an even larger monetary award for each patient admitted with the disease, and even if they did not, they were still recorded as having it. It was all part of the bonus pay out plan, because the larger number of patients coming in with the disease added an extra incentive for people to get the injections.

It was a successful plan as more and more people readily stood in long lines to get more of the injections. They were getting more of the deadly injections they trusted would help them. But, Jules knew better, as did her Pleiadian team, and they were taking notes.

It was obvious to Jules that the mandated injections were causing the very serious side effects patients were coming in with. Thousands of people were reporting serious side effects after being injected. But they were two brainwashed to put two and two together. Jules heard all sorts of horrible stories. For example, a husband could get the injection, come home and drop death in front of his wife with a heart attack, and his mind controlled, brainwashed, wife would never put two and two together. She would just think he died of a heart attack and of course the medical people would not tell her anything else, such as the injection he just received was the evil culprit; although they definitely knew better.

For the people were successfully media brainwashed to believe that the injections were wonderful life saving tools in their arsenal of the modern-day drug and medical system. Jules, continued to contact and update Wisdom.

Wisdom, was a teleporting Pleiadian star seed from Alcyone, the brightest star of the Pleiades constellation. She is called Wisdom by her commander, Serena, and her peers, because she was at the top of her rank, wise and very knowledgeable in all things about the Galactic Federation. The Galactic Federation is made up of more than two-hundred planetary bodies of the Galactic universe. They all came together in defense against the evil Reptilian population and had entrapped them in the third dimensional matrix of Verda. They did not want to involve the humans on Verda, but they felt they had no choice. The Reptiles were evil and had to be contained. They had been attacking and destroying other planets in the universe. All the rest of the universe is of the fifth dimension of universal consciousness and love, except for the evil Reptilian race.

Nearly twelve thousand years ago, the Taygetans, from Taygeta a star planet in the Pleiades star system, went along with the rest of the Galactic Federation and installed a computer on Verda's moon that would project and transpose a third dimensional matrix of the existing fifth dimension of Verda. The plan was to contain the evil war mongering reptilians there on Verda. The computer is very old and is failing. At the time, the idea was to contain the Reptilians on Verda's third dimension until the debris in the universe cleared up. The debris was everywhere after the evil reptilians blew up planet Telemer in a clandestine ambush operation, that the Reptilians had set up in an effort to destroy Taygeta.

Wisdom, a pretty blue-eyed, tall woman with long wavy blonde hair had a determined mind, and had a certain sway to her walk that proved it. Wisdom is a star seed Pleiadian born on Verda; but easily teleports between Verda and Taygeta. As Pleiadian human hybrid she is on Verda as a watcher from the Galactic Federation. She has the capacity to teleport as a spiritual being between planet Verda and Taygeta of the Pleiades star system.

Wisdom has been assigned to planet Verda by her commander, Serena. Serena is the high priestess of Taygeta. Serena's position is one of the highest ranking positions of the Galactic Federation, a lead commander. It is her job to see that the Pleiadians protect the planets of the universe from harmful Reptilian predators. Bad things were happening on planet Verda since the human hating evil Reptilians stole DNA from humans and created shape shifting reptilian humanoid hybrids who had infiltrated with the humans on the surface of Verda. Their purpose was to mingle with the humans and take over by ruthlessly scratching and clawing their way to the top positions of corporations and government. Their goal was to cause havoc, chaos, and human annihilation, even if it took the total destruction of Verda.

They were successful as the government was bought and run by greedy corporate interests. And the vicious shape shifting reptilian humanoid hybrids only used people for their monetary gain, medical experiments, satanic rituals, and depopulation purposes. They manipulated and tricked the people into compliancy by inadvertently mass programming and brainwashing them through media lies and propaganda.

The reptilian humanoid hybrids raised up from the abyss of hell in the center of Verda, rose to the top echelon and elbowed their way into every powerful position of corporations and government. The population of Verda was doomed and aimed for demise, unless quick action was to take place and rid Verda of all the evil energies of the reptilians humanoid hybrids--fast, before they succeeded in destroying all human life on planet Verda.

The evil ones easily clawed their way to the top of the drug industries where they created degenerating diseases and made them airborne. When people became ill, they visited medical facilities for help. They left with a Band-Aid on their arm after receiving an injection, and carried with them a handful of various prescriptions for pills, claimed as remedies, but were actually toxic pills that would eventually end up making them feel worse. And so the maiming continued.

When the evil ones thought people were not responding to their media suggestions fast enough, they merely came up with another threat of another even more dangerous spreading disease that would be so deadly they felt they had to make the injections mandatory. Loudspeakers were installed and used in every heavily populated area. Angry sounding male authoritarian voices were used to trigger certain frequencies that revved up the intensity in the nano particle microchips that had already been implanted by the injections. Certain key words and voice tones triggered certain frequencies and made the chip injected victims even more docile and zombie like. The order to receive another round of injections was screamed out from the loudspeakers, and demanded people get in line, roll up their sleeves and get their injections. With loudspeakers and monitors situated on every corner, they screamed the danger of the disease saying that it would cause great debilitating harm or even death.

Passing through building walls in spirit form, and going through medical facility records, Wisdom noticed that most of the people got the disease after they got the mandated injections. Looking even further into some hidden files and records coming from all medical facilities in Malcatraz, and from all of Verda, Wisdom discovered that millions of people were experiencing injuries after receiving the injections, and some were becoming disabled. And she discovered there had already been more than a million who had dropped dead from sudden heart failure, within a few hours after they received the injections. She was appalled to learn this. The side effects were not slight or temporary but were debilitating and horrendous. The toxic reptilian humanoid hybrid run medical industry, was keeping it secret.

Tthe nano particle microchips in the injections had brainwashed people and programmed them not to be able to put two and two together, so they were rendered with brain fog and totally clueless as to where the real danger lay, and that was in the toxic injections.

Passed souls of the victims, who crossed over the veil into the ether of the universe, clearly saw what led to their demise. They were angry and hung around, and watched, and waited for their chance to retaliate their revenge. As the groups of passed souls grew, they became more upset and angry by the leaders deceit and evil depopulation program. And on the other side of the veil, these passed humans now in their soul, spiritual forms, saw that the heads of corporations and government were evil reptiles transformed into shape shifting reptilian humanoid hybrids in order to fool and entrap the humans into their plans of total demise.

The evil shape shifting reptilian humanoid hybrids were crafty and smooth in their brainwashing techniques. And the passed human spirits felt they had been tricked and murdered, and they wanted their lives back. Since transforming from the physical back into spiritual beings on the other side, they saw and heard everything that was truly going on behind the scenes back on planet Verda.

They were angry, and they wanted revenge on the three well known scientists and ringleaders Dewy, Cheatem, and Howd. They were angry to have been tricked and murdered by their very own government. After the deceased passed across the veil, they could then see the truth. They had been mandated to be injected with a known dangerous and potentially fatal drug that was deliberately created to depopulate most of planet Verda. They felt it was a lie and a murderous scam.

The thousands of passed souls were indeed cheated needlessly out of their futures, unable to fulfill their dreams, and they were irate. It was mass murder at best, and on the other side, the victims learned the evil truth of the depopulation scam. They saw who they were and learned the leaders of corporate back fascist government and top positions in corporations were actually ruthless and vicious reptilian humanoid hybrids wanting to rid planet Verda of all the humans, because they wanted Verda all to themselves. They were murderers without consciousness, without souls, and they only knew hate and to instill fear into the humans.

The passed spirits of the victims, also learned that the ruthless reptilian humanoid hybrids carried on their pure blood reptile desire for adrenaline charged frightened blood of the very young and most tender humans. The evil flesh eaters frightened their prey to near death before sacrificing them in the process of drinking their young adrenaline super-charged blood. And yes the practice went on behind the scenes in secret satanic rituals by members of the highest positions of the corporate infused fascist government of Verda.

The passed souls now knew the truth, and were angry, and revengeful and demanded retaliation. From across the veil they plotted revenge to expose what was occurring on planet Verda. They were geared to expose the reptilian humanoid hybrid's secret depopulation plan that was planned to have the murders appear on death certificates as death by natural or unknown causes.

"Evidently they made the injections too toxic," Jules reported to Wisdom, "What was supposed to be slow looking natural deaths were beginning to look like intended deaths." Jules teleported mind to mind to Wisdom the information and then made plans that were telepathically transported mind to mind to and from the many souls of the passed victims.

"Wisdom, these passed victims souls are irate," Jules reported, "and they vow to get revenge on the elites who planned the scam disease and the mandated toxic injections."

The sudden deaths made it quite obvious to Jules that the injection manufacturers overlooked the fact that toxic polyethylene glycol, an oil product used in antifreeze, was already manufactured into many pills, injections and food products. Many humans already had a toxic allergic build up, so when a sudden burst of it was injected directly into their bodies with a needle, they soon collapsed dead from anaphylactic shock.

"What do these passed victims plan on doing?" Wisdom urgently asked becoming more curious by the second. Being in the Galactic Federation for a long time, she had never experienced such a horrid attempt of total annihilation of the whole human race. She was appalled of the secrecy, as previous wars amongst nations were blatant and out in the open. This was a secretive, seditious, vicious, and horrendous act.

"I can overhear telepathic mind to mind messages between these young passed souls of athletics. They are planning a mass revenge tactic on the corporate backed fascist government leaders and planners of the whole scam, especially the three main developers, Dewy, Cheatem and Howd and their team of initiators behind the whole toxic scheme to depopulate the planet of Verda," reported Jules.

"Such an audacious, cowardly act by these three evil ones," stated Wisdom. "I do not blame any of the victims who want revenge. I firmly believe these vicious reptilian humanoid hybrid males need to be exposed, so the humans know the truth. Then the evil ones need to be exposed in compliance with Galactic Federation rules, which in this case calls for the upmost strictest capital punishment, slow death by fright."

"I think spiritual being revenge is the best way to retaliate, After all, what do these passed souls have to lose? They certainly can't be murdered, again. A soul is pure energy that cannot be disposed, unlike evil reptilians who have no soul, no moral compass, and only know to conquer, promote fear and murder," interjected Jules. "When the third dimensional matrix encompassing Verda is no longer, and the computer on Verda's moon is been shut down, the evil reptilians will die. They cannot survive outside the third dimension; the reptilians and their reptilian humanoid hybrids will perish if they have not already been frightened to death by revengeful murdered spiritual beings."

"I think it is brilliant and well serving," said Wisdom.

"These passed soul spirits can easily appear anywhere in a thought and pass easily through structures, walls and doors."

Wisdom, and Jules were amongst the women of Taygeta of the Pleiades where there are mostly women and very few males. The women of the Pleiades are not fans of patriarchal authoritarian rule, nor males in general. So women run the government and make all the decisions. The males tend to domestic duties. And yes, it is the reverse of planet Verda, where misogynistic, narcissistic, egotistical reptilian humanoid hybrids males initiated patriarchal rule which has always been the dominating factor, and subsequently, has also nearly ruined planet Verda because of the shape shifting reptilian humanoid hybrids' greed, evil, absence of conscience, and lack of heart and soul. The misogynistic, egotistical, narcissistic reptilian humanoid hybrids have been running things on Verda for thousands of years. It's time the third dimensional matrix bubble burst, so love and generosity of the fifth dimension is allowed to rebirth Verda into a planet of love and healing.

"Frankly, I think it will be the only way justice will be served," Jules said, "as all the law, courts, governments, and the medical and drug cooperate heads are all obviously in on it. Many have been tricked into participating in satanic rituals and then blackmailed into committing these atrocities. It all has been witnessed and recorded, according to the passed murdered victims who see all, past, present, and future now from the other side of the veil, and they telepathically report it all to me. They are in the process of frightening the reptilian humanoid hybrids now, to expose them for what they truly are, evil shape shifting reptilian humanoid hybrids. This type of a tit for tat revengeful act is justified as the murdered victims trusted the establishment and did not see their attacks coming. Nor will these evil reptilian humanoid hybrids see the revengeful spiritual beings coming to show themselves and to frighten the evil ones as they do not believe in spirit souls, or life after death.

"So when the reptilians die, that will be the end of them. In the spirit world, humans are spiritual beings, experiencing life on planet Verda as human beings. They were spiritual beings before they incarnated on Verda, and they will be spiritual beings when their bodies die and they cross back over the veil. The evil reptilians do not have a conscience, but all other living things have a conscience, be it plant, mineral, animal or human, they are conscience spiritual energy, and energy never dies. The evil reptilians do not have this, and they do not believe in the spirit world, nor mind to mind connection, as spiritual beings do, and are all part of the collective consciousness of the universe. And now even more so, we are all connected since Verda has entered the rim of the fifth dimension rejoining the rest of the universe."

"Well, the reptilians cannot survive out of the third or fourth dimension, certainly not the fifth, so they will die out, it's enviable as soon as the third dimensional matrix veil is totally lifted," said Wisdom with a slight smile. "Finally, the Galactic Confederation can soon close this case and Verda can become the planet it was always meant to be, with organic rich soils for planting, clear blue skies, clean fresh air, and clear fresh water abound."

"Humans on Verda have suffered long enough. It's time for spiritual justice to be carried out," smiled Jules.

"I just got a telepathic update from the passed soul athletic sports players who had been injection murdered and crossed the veil," said Wisdom. "They said their large group of the souls of passed victims appeared to the ringleaders Dewy, Cheatem and Howd who were having a televised meeting with other high officials on their team."

"What did they say?" ask Jules. She couldn't wait to hear the answer.

"That we will see the effects of their efforts by way of nearly frightened to death signs of bulging eyes, and when they speak their voices will stutter and shake, as will soon be seen on all televised monitor tubes. It happened in full view of the public while being televised across all of Verda.

The passed spirits of the athletics frightened them just as they gathered in the network studio and stood behind microphones and in front of the live televised cameras. The passed spirits zipped by, hovered, and howled in their faces, frightening them so badly that their eyes turned to reptilian yellow vertical slits and they shape shifted from human appearing reptilian humanoid hybrids back to pure reptilians out of fear, right in front of a live broadcast and with cameras recording.

"The studio audience gasped as the evil reptilian humanoid hybrids lost control of their shape shifting abilities to disguise themselves and appear human. And their true reptilian selves emerged for all of Verda to see in their true form, growing huge and bursting out of their business suits. Human screams could be heard across the nations of Verda.

"Then, for all humans to see, the evil reptiles suddenly turned to a dark crystallized dust and dissipated into thin air as the computer on Verda's moon suddenly shut down completely, ending the rein of human terror, as the third dimensional matrix Verda was trapped in ended. Verda was once again in the fifth dimension. The terror on Verda had suddenly ended as the evil reptilian turned to dust and drifted away into the ether of faraway universes. In a mist of dust, their evil energies dissipated and evaporated into total nothingness," Wisdom reported gleefully.

All on Verda slowly recovered from the shock of what they had just witnessed. The news channels were bursting with the news that Dewy, Cheatem and Howd, and other members of their team, confessed to everything and the whole planet of Verda witnessed it. It was as if they had consumed truth serum. The evil ones revealed everything, and it was all recorded, confessing to knowing pills and injections were lethal to depopulate Verda of humans.

People shook with fear, as the group appeared shift

changed from human back into pure reptilian creatures. Their sudden monstrous appearances had frightened the directors, producers, and camera operators. Many ran out of the building frightened and shocked at the huge monsters that suddenly appeared before them. But the frightened shaking, even screaming, dedicated cameraman remained at their stations. Some televised portions were so shaky that many people watching, even though they were icky and got motion sickness, kept watching. Some members of the studio audience ran, and in their efforts to get away, were knocking over equipment and bursting out into the streets.

For weeks the people of Verda relived the horrendous moments repeatedly, watching over and over again the recorded televised events. The reptiles stood in full view before the cameras and microphones, that cut in and out but still picked up the other worldly deep throated roars of the huge raging scaly and green, short armed, long swirling tailed, big tooth, roaring reptilians. It all happened so suddenly after the computer on Verda's moon totally shut down and the third dimension ceased to exist.

All of Verda returned to the fifth dimension, and cheers were heard around the planet of Verda. Humans sang praise as those physically maimed by all the toxic pills and injections were suddenly healed, no longer brainwashed and mind controlled as computer chips dissolved. Verda was now a loving paradise. The third dimensional bubble had disappeared, and Verda was now back into the fifth dimension of total love.

The historical events had been recorded, as a lesson never to forget witnessing the wisp of spirit dust drifting in front of them as the reptiles, shaking with fright, than devolved, dissipated, and disappeared. It was the passed victims spirits showing themselves to the evil reptiles that frightened them out of existence. It was a sight no one will ever forget as the ringleaders, Dewy, Cheatem, and Howd, while still in reptilian humanoid hybrid form were up front, in the spotlight, speaking into the microphones with cameras zoomed in close. And then seeing Dewy, Cheatem, and Howd's eyes suddenly bulge out, grew large and suddenly returned to reptilian yellow vertical slit eyes. A cameraman's screams could be heard as Dewy, Cheatem and Howd, shift changed from appearing human, to turning completely back into reptiles in full reptilian form with green scaly bodies, talons, long tails, growling with sharp teeth showing.

More screams could be heard. All of their team on stage followed Dewy, Cheatem, and Howd, and shift changed back into full reptiles. The camera lens shook, and the televised picture coming across was blurry and shook a bit. Another cameraman eager to record the excitement of the moment, quickly turned and focused his camera on the frightened people running out of the room, then swung back suddenly to where there were at least eight huge reptiles standing in front of the cameras. The producers who were too frightened to run out of the studio, along with the cameramen and operators caught the slight glimpse of a group of passed souls' spirit dust, sparkling and whirling and dancing in the air, as the past souls floated pass between the cameras and the reptiles. At the same time, the moon computer shut down and ended the third dimension. Across the whole planet of Verda, every evil reptilian humanoid hybrid shift changed back to full reptilian before dissipated into the fifth dimension into nothingness.

As the citizens all over the planet of Verda were watching on their televisions, they experienced a live transformation from human form back to reptilian form right before their very eyes. It was recorded and caught on tape as the live news show was being broadcast. Suddenly as if the Galactic Federation computer on Verda's moon had blown a fuse, it shut down, and the third dimension was no longer. Verda was back in the fifth dimension.

Not being able to withstand the atmospheric change from twenty percent oxygen and eight percent nitrogen to eighty percent oxygen and twenty percent nitrogen, the reptilians suddenly collapsed to the floor, struggling to breath they appeared to be dying, then quickly turned to dust and disappeared into nothingness. The computer on Verda's moon totally shut down and Verda was back into the fifth dimension and finally rid of all of the evil reptiles.

People suddenly had seen on television just what evil lurked in high ruling positions. It could not have happened any better than that. There can be no misbeliefs or accusations of mistrust when it happens in front of people's very eyes.

# *Chapter Seventeen*

CHEERS COULD BE HEARD coming from everywhere around the planet of Verda; it was as if a horrifying veil had been lifted and indeed it had. Everyone was dancing in the streets. Back into the fifth dimension, there was mass healing. All the maimed victims who had shaking nervous conditions, and any other horrific side effects from the injections, were suddenly totally cured, when the atmosphere of Verda switched from the oxygen starved third dimension back into the plenty of oxygen fifth dimension. Suddenly too, there was a sense of well-being and the feeling of love permeated the planet. Everyone praised and thanked the passed souls of the athletics and other passed injection victims who returned to physical human form. They gathered to cheer on as the athletes returned to their soccer fields in control of their human lives living their dreams.

Verda was finally back to the fifth dimension after hundreds of thousands of years of being trapped along with the reptiles in the third dimension. In the fifth dimension the veil was much thinner between the spiritual beings and the spiritual beings in physical human form on Verda. With the veil much thinner, the spirit beings on the other side could communicate mind to mind telepathically much easier across the veil. Everyone on Verda was now realizing their own psychic powers and abilities. Their remote viewing and clairvoyance abilities, that was always there, but humans were never permitted to know that. Patriarchal rule of the reptilians humanoid hybrids wanted them dumbed down and totally dependent on them for all of their needs.

The spirits of the athletic players had played their best game yet. They and the rest of Verda were rejoicing. They had succeeded in frightening the reptilian humanoid hybrids in to revealing their true selves. Verda was free, and now in the fifth dimension of universal knowledge and love. In the fifth dimension, passed over spirits could enjoy and easily connect with their living loved ones on Verda as the veil between the physical and the spiritual had thinned.

# Chapter Eighteen

MEDICAL WORKERS WHO REFUSED the mandated injections, and were fired, had formed many holistic healing centers all over Malcatraz and the rest of Verda. In the fifth dimension, they were free to specialize in helping victims to further heal to full recovery, and heal their bodies in organic natural ways from the horrendous side effects of the toxic injections. Many of the victims had horrible nerve damage from the injections and as they ate organic foods and used essential oils, walked on the grass, and sat in the sunshine and meditated, their conditions rapidly improved. It was as if all of Verda was born again.

With great loving care, the planting soil was restored to organic mineral richness. Organic plants grew everywhere. Bees returned to carry pollen nectar between flowering plants. The sun shone bright as clear crystal in a clear blue sky and the horrible chem trails were never seen again. The citizens of planet Verda were returning to good health merely by having toxic chemicals in the form of pills or injections cleared from their systems with pure clean water, clean air, and organic food.

They learned that they could self-health with a nourished immune system. They learned that love and their very minds controlled their health; that positive thoughts created positive health and a positive reality. There was no crime on Verda; everyone worked together for the greater good to dispose of toxic materials and rebuild their cities and countries with natural organic material. All chemical laboratories and factories were safety disposed of. Oceans were cleaned up of all plastics; any toxic oil products were cleaned up and safely disposed of. All the people on Verda united and thought of themselves as one continuous family.

They discovered that without the evil-minded reptilian humanoid hybrids running corporate backed governments that there were no quarrels, no disputes. No pitting one nation against another. Verda was a total democracy with a two-party system but with each party wanting the same outcomes and goals, only with different ideas of ways for achieving them. So the end goal was the same. There was love and respect for everyone.

Religion was replaced with spirituality. There was no discrepancy between races, and finally there was equality between men and women. Each loved and respected the other gender. After having such an evil horrible existence on Verda, present and future generations would be constantly reminded of what once was and determined never to be again. People on Verda were more creative and creativity was encouraged by all.

All vehicles were solar powered, and abandoned pyramids positioned throughout Verda were once again activated and generated natural cost-free electricity and used all over the planet of Verda. Finally, people were free to use the power of the pyramids as they had been meant to be used as the ancients had intended. They were now used as they were used in ancient times as free zero-point energy power plants, just as the benevolent extraterrestrials who built and designed them intended them to be used--to provide free electricity for everyone on the whole planet of Verda.

With the reptiles gone, greed was gone. There was no such thing as hate, greed, or conquering fear, as that was gone away with, when the evil reptilians perished. Verda was the pristine paradise it was meant to be. All the huge amounts of monies that the evil reptilian humanoid hybrids acquired from their wretched ways, was redistributed back to the people. Since most items were designed and hand crafted, and food was grown in individual gardens, not much money was needed. And when it was needed, prices were very reasonable and fair. So the money the reptilian humanoid hybrids had stored up was all evenly distributed to all the people of Verda. There was so much of it and prices were so fair and reasonable that no one had to work for anyone else but themselves; enjoying being artistic, creative, and sharing. People traded and bought and sold amongst themselves.

People were grateful to be free to be themselves and gift their artsy talents to society in the form of creative architecture using all natural and organic materials. Plastic like materials were created from various types of plant oils and wood. With everything being natural and organic, the planet of Verda was healing fast as were its occupants.

The soil was enriched and smelled fresh and clean as was the waterways, and birds sang praise. People held drumming ceremonies and honored and praised the soil, wind, sun, sky and cherished the clean rains. The night sky was so clean and pure without jet fuel and toxic chem trails, that nightly star viewing was the most popular evening activity accompanied by sounds of classical music, flute playing and drumming.

Since there was no evil reptilian humanoid hybrids spewing negative propaganda and driving the forces of hate between people, there was no hate, only love and respect all around. And good loving energy everywhere made the planet even more rich in human, plant and animal life.

There was still some, but less and less animal protein eaten; although it was raised humanly and naturally and grass fed. But, most animals were seen as pets because humans realized that all living creatures were created with a never dying soul, as spirit is eternal energy, and energy never dies.

Humans were living much longer, and when after

nearly two hundred years of living when someone chose to pass across the veil, it was a planned event and ceremonial. With such love all around, humans easily rose up to higher dimensions than the fifth dimension. They could easily teleport themselves to other star systems and back again merely by using their thoughts, their minds. Humans had been hidden from these facts; it was their time now to explore the powers and capabilities of their minds. They found their minds to be very powerful for self-healing and the healing of others; as our minds our all connected by the universal mind, our power source of the consciousness of our souls.

Now humans were free to live up to their best and full potentials. In the cities buildings were tall and spiral and made of crystal for memory and electoral storage strength. Crystal was used to store knowledge and circulate natural electricity. The arts were the most important things now on Verda as creative art is spiritual and healing. Music and art were taught by everyone. People created, traded and sold things, and shared knowledge.

Everyone had personal size anti-gravity vehicles. There was anti-gravity vehicle parking docks on every balcony, alongside vertical gardens, of the high rise skyscrapers in the center of cities where people lived, gathered, dinned out and socialized. Everyone in their personal zero point anti-gravity silent space vehicles traveled all over Verda to different countries and even ventured out into space to visit other planets.

# *Chapter Nineteen*

WISDOM WAS UPDATED by the revengeful passed spirits of the athletics now back in human form. They were thrilled they got their revenge on the reptilians, the reptilian humanoid hybrids, and made them come clean and expose their true selves while on a media interview for all of Verda to see. These passed spirits are happy that Verda is in the fifth dimension and that the veil between the physical and spiritual was thinned, so that spiritual beings and spiritual beings in human form are one step closer to the spiritual realm and can interact more easily. Wisdom now felt she had two homes that she lived, the Pleiades and Verda.

Wisdom, updated Serena that the governments of the nations of Verda were in the process of being overhauled with the way being paved by a large group of passed spirit heroes. They were victims of the injections, but they no longer felt cheated out of a physical life, as they had helped saved the planet of Verda from being totally destroyed by the evil reptilians.

All on Verda never forgot what was and would never

be allowed again as Wisdom reported to Serena. Verda had entered a time of the Aquarian fifth dimension of feminine energy and rule by their loving forces. Wisdom and her crew that were infiltrated throughout planet Verda witnessed the dawning of a new day for Verda as the planet had turned into an organic paradise and wonderful happy healthy people were loving and helping each other out as they had a heart and consciousness that the reptilian human hybrids failed to destroy in the people of planet Verda.

The patriarchal rule of the third dimension had ended on planet Verda. Wisdom and her crew that included the passed injected victims spirits had help to end the disaster. Planet Verda had been a prison planet, where the dark and evil reptilian humanoid hybrids were trapped under a third dimensional matrix on planet Verda when the ancient twelve-thousand-year-old computer placed on the artificial moon of Verda placed there by the Galactic Federation to rein in all the evil reptilians on Verda.

# *Chapter Twenty*

SOON, IT WAS GLOBAL, the truth was out to all the population of planet Verda, that the evil without soul or conscious reptilian human hybrids that had been running corporate backed government with the goal of depopulation. As the evil reptilians' goal was to rid Verda of all human except for a few million human slaves to do their bidding.

"So, Wisdom, what happened to Dewy, Cheatem and Howd?" Serena wanted to know.

Wisdom reported that a team of passed soccer players gave them a rough time. "They appeared to them and frightened them into staring wide-eyed space and crippled in place," reported Wisdom

"What?" asked Serena.

"They completely lost their minds," reported Wisdom. "The soccer players also appeared to each of the corporate heads too. Evidently none of them had ever seen ghosts before," smiled Wisdom.

"The Galactic Federation have followed the passed spirits lead and have totally shut down the third dimensional matrix veil that was entrapping the reptilian human hybrids and humans together on Verda. The fleeing reptilians all dissipated into nothingness when the fifth dimension was restored to Verda.

The Galactic Federation set up bases around Verda to help the humans restore the constitution of democracy governments. Humans were free from all mandating pill and jabs and restrictions. They were free to restore the soil and grow all organic plants, the sky was a beautiful blue since all of toxic chem trails were stopped. The planet was blooming. The humans were joyous to smell the fresh soil of Verda and eat its glorious vegetables and fruits. The humans of Verda united and rejoiced their newfound freedoms. The planet was totally organic, and everyone wanted it that way.

With the evil reptilians gone out of existence, the humans of Verda united in love and freedom and cooperation. With the evil reptilians cast out to their deaths, Verda was a living paradise of peace love and harmony in all of the countries Verda. Verda became very futuristic and actually caught up with other futuristic constellations in the universe that made up the Galactic Federation.

Anti-gravity space craft easily traveled thoroughout the universe trading ideas, goods and services, a fifth dimension universe of love and harmony. Most importantly the humans on Verda were perfectly healthy as they were happy, calm, relaxed, loving, enjoying clean air, clean water, organic foods and no toxic chemical infused genetically modified organisms fake foods, or lethal drugs or jabs; so there was literally no illness and humans lived active healthy lives to be until nearly two-hundred years old or longer, if they wished before their spirits left their physical bodies and ascended back into their spiritual form. They themselves chose when they wanted to pass into the spiritual realm.

All the young sports players and other people whose bodies beating hearts were murdered by the toxic reptilian humanoid hybrid evil scams reincarnated as adults back on planet Verda. The soccer and other sports players were back to play in physical form.

Now the humans on Verda had total free will over their own bodies, as a gift from the fifth dimension, and all the soul spirits whose lives were cut short due to being entrapped on Verda's third dimensional prison planet. Now they had the choice to revisit their past lives on Verda, back to right where they left off, or create another physical life on Verda adventure, only this time, without the evil demented dangerous evil reptilian humanoid hybrids roaming Verda.

Back in the glorious fifth dimension there was no greedy elite or ruling class. Everyone was created equal, unlike planet Earth that ended up being destroyed by the evil reptilian humanoid hybrids that ruled there. The humans that had escaped the toxic medical system were rescued by the humans of Verda who came and got them in their anti-gravity crafts while Earth crumbled into an antiqued heap of toxic oil machines, just as the evil reptilians had left the uninhabitable sand pits of

Mars behind before the Galactic Federation managed to trap them on Verda.

After the evil reptilians were destroyed throughout the universe, the Galactic Federation realized they should have done it thousands of years ago, destroy them, instead of entrapping them on planet Verda in the third dimension with innocent humans. But a lesson came out of it and that was love rules the universe, and that humans are spirit beings with hearts of love and consciousness experiencing life as human beings never to take it for granted.

*Verda* is Dianne Zimmermann's eighth fictional novel. Dianne shares her time between St. Louis and Sedona. She is an Alcyone, Pleiadian star seed psychic medium and enjoys writing, drawing, photography, biking, hiking, and road trips. She enjoys performing at open mic events as "DianneZ and her Ukulele" the lounge singer. She croons the old standard favorites in her unique style singing and playing her ukulele. She can be contacted at DianneTheMedium.com for zoom mediumship readings and singing and playing engagements. Dianne not only enjoys singing but also listening to herself talk, you can too, listen at *DianneTheMedium* podcast at PodBean.

www.ingramcontent.com/pod-product-compliance
Lightning Source LLC
LaVergne TN
LVHW041947070526
838199LV00051BA/2927